The Naked Tuck Shop

Growing up gay in the 1950s

Tim Hughes

The Naked Tuck Shop
Growing up gay in the 1950s

© Tim Hughes 2019.

Acknowledgements
I would like to thank Peter J Robinson Jnr for allowing me to use his photo of Enrique, and Adam D'Oyly John for the use of the back cover photograph; all my dear departed friends and mentors, without whom this memoir would not exist; and my special Black Country friend who has given me the encouragement and help to complete it. Some names have been changed for obvious reasons.

ISBN 978-1-78222-712-0

Book production and distribution management by Into Print
www.intoprint.net
+44 (0)1604 832149

For Enrique Luna, RIP

I would still have loved you as Henry Moon

Contents

Young hearts run free
be true to yourself
never be hung-up

Candi Staton

Preface

The Naked Tuck Shop is a memoir of my teenage years as a
boarder at the Royal Grammar School in Colchester and prior
to that at Whitchurch House Preparatory School for Boys in
Oxfordshire. We had been living abroad in Cyprus and Egypt
as my father was stationed until 1955 in Egypt's Canal Zone,
then under British rule and just prior to the Suez Crisis. When
I was eleven my parents decided the time had come to pack me
off to England to complete my education as 'a young gentleman
of the ruling classes'.

Portions of this memoir have already appeared in gay
periodicals. It is explicit and I believe of historic interest. Above
all, it is my own take on 'gaiety' long before it was legal, or
accepted by British society. I have used the term 'gay'
throughout, although it was not in general use in 1950s
Britain. 'Queer' was the more familiar but derogatory term –
but by the 1960s 'gay', a recent American import, began to be
used as both a noun and adjective in describing homosexuals
and their lifestyle.

I was lucky to recognise and embrace my gayness at a very
early age, and fortunate to be mentored from the age of fourteen,
with very few outright predatory advances, by a group of
extraordinary older gay men. Some of them were celebrated in
various fields – in an age long before 'celebrity' was catnip to the
tell-all tabloids and in the present day our all-intrusive social
media. Discreet homosexual relationships and behaviours could
be lived in relative privacy in those days. My 'new family' showed
me by example the utterly wonderful holistic worth of a gay life –
despite the prevalence of homophobia and a distinctly non-gay
friendly outside world.

Many of these men remained close friends until their eventual
passing.

Through them I discovered a vast clandestine and fascinating world that stretched through all levels of society – from peers of the realm, to long distance lorry drivers. For me it was a tremendously exciting and happy experience growing-up gay in the late 1950s and early 1960s – although I recognise in retrospect that I was blessed and that for many teens it was, and still remains, even in today's supposedly enlightened times, sheer agony.

Tim Hughes, 2019

1. Voyages

I was eleven in the summer of 1954 and my parents decided it was high time to send me back to Prep School in England. We were living in Egypt. My RAF officer father was stationed in the Canal Zone, which at that time prior to the Suez Crisis was occupied by the British. They took me to Port Said for the long sea voyage back to Southampton. It had been arranged for me to be under the temporary guardianship of a military family who were also returning to England. I shared a small two bunk bed cabin with an ugly, boring boy, who spent the entire voyage making model aeroplanes – a hobby that held little interest for an artistic lad like myself. The all pervading smell of Airfix glue in that confined space was unbearable and so I escaped to the upper decks, even sleeping there at times if the weather was warm. Years later in New York, in one of my first forays into 'chemsex lite', a trick I picked up on the piers at the bottom of Christopher Street introduced me to the dangerous and head shaking delights of glue sniffing.

Lightly chaperoned by my *in loco parentis* keepers – who in any case were preoccupied with their own four boisterous kids – I had one fleeting homoerotic attempt from a ship's steward. I had noticed him eying me up for days. Then one morning he rubbed himself up against me passing in the ship's narrow passageway. Picky, even at that young age, I did not find his attempt at *frottage*, or him, particularly alluring. He clocked this and his advances were never repeated. Looking back it was more a case of my later friend Peggy Mount's hit play, *Sailor Beware*, than 'Hello Sailor' – that camp nautical greeting popularised by those bona boys, Julian and Sandy, in the equally camp classic 1960s radio show, *Round the Horne*.

My first significant sexual experience had actually happened the year before in Egypt. Confined to bed with chicken pox I was home alone in the sweltering Egyptian summer heat.

Military housing quarters had no such luxury as AC. I was lying on my bed under the ceiling fan clad only in my underpants, when in the manner of those far-off colonial days, our houseboy Mohammed came in to clean the room. He was only sixteen – utterly charming and quite fascinating. The family, my parents and my brother, were initially aghast at some

Me with my brother and Mum – not quite Omar Sharif.

of his strange customs. One was to pile all his food courses on to one large dinner plate, when after serving at table he retired to the kitchen to eat his own meal. Gravy on top of trifle was particularly grotesque looking. The other most notable trait was his exotic brand of dentistry.

When he had been paid at the end of the month, he would

disappear to Cairo for his days off – only to reappear each time with yet another gold tooth. Over time he replaced all his front teeth with gleaming gold ones. It gave him a truly beguiling smile. Mohammed insisted it was much safer than putting his savings in an Egyptian bank. I asked him one day, what would happen if he was run over by a bus – that would be just *kismet* (fate), he shrugged.

That hot steamy afternoon Mohammed seemed distracted by my lack of clothes and I was suddenly aware of a distinctly developing bulge under his *jalaba*, the traditional white robe worn by Arab men. Intrigued, I asked him what it was? He came over to the bed and raised the robe to display a very erect but scarred brown cock. I had never seen a circumcised cock before – in this case, butchered would really be a better description. This was the result, I found out later, of the less then professional surgery carried out by Egyptian village barbers. Barbers across the world were traditionally the first surgeons as well – as denoted by the blood red and white stripy pole they used to have outside their shops.

His dick resembled nothing like the flawlessly 'cut' gay men I met in New York – where American post-war ideas of 'proper' penile hygiene, reinforced by Jewish religious rules, or indeed the preponderance of Jewish paediatricians, still held sway. Indeed my fortuitously retained foreskin was much prized in the States. Today the preference for an 'uncut dick' is all too obviously stated in the majority of profiles on gay internet dating sites.

Mohammed was equally surprised by my intact foreskin and told me he had never seen one before. He then showed me how to masturbate and I was very aroused by the sight of his ejaculate. I felt no sense of shame at this my introduction to homosex – it just seemed natural to me.

He lived in a tent in our garden and I soon got into the habit of stealing out late at night, when the family was fast asleep, to visit my new friend for a spot of erotic fun. Sadly all this came to an abrupt end, when one day I foolishly told my brother about Mohammed's circumcision. He duly reported this to my parents and the poor lad was immediately sent packing. For ages I felt profoundly guilty for his dismissal.

I am a firm believer in the theories of the Nobel Prize winning animal behaviourist, Konrad Lorenz, and his study of 'imprinting'. He demonstrated how baby animals automatically adopt a close bond with their very first caregiver – in his case studies these were infant animals adopted by a human. My primary erotic arousal was with a brown lad – so was 'imprinting' the reason I have always preferred to choose men of colour to be my lovers and sex partners?

Back to that long voyage home. It took two long weeks with a short stop-off in Malta. My maternal grandmother was waiting for me at Southampton to take me to her home in nearby Winchester. From then on I would spend all my school holidays with Nan until my parents returned to England. She really doted on her favourite grandson. In retrospect I see I took way too much advantage of her. It shames me now to have to admit that although I was perfectly capable of doing so myself she would polish my shoes and make my bed every morning. I never protested. Was this a result of her own Lorenzian imprinting experience – behaviour learned through years of running behind upper-class public school boys and being treated like a skivvy in her housekeeping work at Winchester College?

Soon after my arrival she took me by train to Reading to get me kitted out for my Prep School. In those far-off days, long before Tesco cut-priced and homogenised even something as utilitarian as school uniforms, one obtained the requisite clothes at a specialist school outfitters. The list of essential clothing sent ahead by Whitchurch House School was immense and probably costly.

First on the list, a green blazer. Then six cotton vests and underpants. Two pairs of grey worsted short trousers; four Winceyette brushed cotton grey shirts; six pairs of long grey socks and a pair of black lace-up shoes. Completing the list was more footwear – pairs of plimsolls, football boots and bedroom slippers. Last but not least, the most expensive item of all, a best

Preparing for the Gymkhana – poor Mum.

grey suit for church on Sundays. All these items, along with four towels, pyjamas and a dressing gown, had to have my name sewn in them for laundry purposes. Nan had already ordered a supply of those now unfamiliar embroidered name tapes, ubiquitous at the time for boarding schools, the military and many other institutions. They must have made a mint for a company with the appropriate name of Cash.

Nan duly took care of this marathon sewing task and I was soon ready to take up my new persona as a 'young gentleman of the ruling classes'. At the end of the summer holidays in

September, we took the train again from Winchester to Reading. Then a taxi to Whitchurch House School, located in the pretty Oxfordshire village of the same name, just across the ancient toll bridge from Pangbourne, for my first term at Prep School.

2. Winchester and the Accident

Nan's house in Winchester was in the precincts of Winchester College, one of England's historic Public Schools for boys.* It was founded six hundred years ago by William of Wyckham, Bishop of Winchester, who was Lord Chancellor to both Edward III and his reputedly gay son, Richard II. Nan was a widow. My grandparents had been employed by the College as domestic servants and it was in the terms of their retirement that faithful employees, for a small rent, could remain living in college property.

The boys enrolled at the school lived in a series of very large Victorian houses each presided over by a housemaster and if married, his wife. My grandfather died of lung cancer in 1947. He was the house butler at Chernocke House, where he met my grandmother who worked in the kitchen.

It all sounds a bit *Downtown Abbey* now, but being in service as it was called was a very common (sic!) profession in those early years of the twentieth century. Granddad, born in Cork, had escaped from hard times in Ireland when he was seventeen to serve in the British Army. He was already widowed when he met Nan, with a brood of six children – aged ten to eighteen. His first wife had died in childbirth. The five girls were also predestined to enter service, as kitchen skivvies, or junior maids by the time they were fifteen. The youngest, an only boy from that first marriage, was already ten when my Mother was born in 1922.

The housemaster, John Bather, had been granddad's commanding officer in the army. He served as his batman – an officer's personal valet drawn from the non-commissioned ranks. Bather's daughter, Elizabeth (Betty), had been a senior officer in

*For Americans, English Public Schools are actually private boarding schools similar to a New England Prep School. The equivalent of your public school is a state school here.

My butler grandfather – Winchester College.

the ATS (later the Women's Royal Army Corps) in the Second World War, subsequently becoming head of the new female division of London's Metropolitan Police Force. She never married but was a closeted lesbian in the old mould. When I met her as a kid she was retired and living with her long-time partner, a Miss Meldrum, who discreetly posed as her lady's companion! One of my aunts, Winnie, was their housekeeper. A big treat in those austere days of post-war rationing, when we visited Nan, was to be invited to Miss Bather's house on Sleeper's Hill for a slap-up cake and cream tea.

One May morning in 1949, when we were staying with Nan, I had a serious accident that profoundly changed the rest of my life.

Directly opposite her house, on Kingsgate Street, were the College sports fields. That morning my brother and I were playing there with Chris, a young boy from further up the street. Chris was my age, just six, and my brother was not yet five. When he was nine Chris would do the real 'Billy Elliot' as a talented working class boy, winning a scholarship to the Royal

Ballet School in London. He graduated to join the company's corps de ballet, where he remained for fifteen years until a long term leg injury finished his dancing career and forced him to retire prematurely. I used to watch him dance regularly, with the free tickets he gave me to the Royal Opera House until I moved to New York in 1972. He was not your stereotype gay ballet boy at all but like 'Billy Elliot' a very sporty hetero. He married another dancer in the company and they moved to Surrey, where she opened a successful children's ballet school, and he bought a vintage car repairs garage.

In the fields that morning a groundsman was cutting the grass on the school cricket pitches with a gang mower – three long rows of rotating blades and metal rollers dragged behind a tractor and little pick-up truck. He asked us kids if we would like to ride in the truck and thrilled we accepted. Standing in the truck my brother and Chris rode facing forward but I stood looking back watching the oily cut grass spray like a rainbow up into the sunlight. The tractor went under a tree. The other two ducked but I was struck in the back of my head by a low hanging branch. I pitched forward head first into the whirling blades of the mower. I bumped my forehead on one of the rollers and bounced free, but unfortunately dragged my left hand through several rows of spinning blades. I will never forget that characteristic smell of oily fresh cut grass and always since then find it difficult to be near anyone mowing.

I lost two of my fingers, half the index finger, and my whole thumb. In those days there were no trained ambulance paramedics rushing to scoop up the amputations and preserve them on ice until they could hopefully be reattached. The bump to the head had made me semi-conscious. I don't remember any pain – just the gruesome sight of a bloody stump where my hand should have been, when I woke up lying in Nan's front room. The desperately upset groundsman had carried me in his arms to the house to await an ambulance.

17

Ahead were three years of multiple surgeries at various hospitals in cities around the country – Winchester, Guildford and Derby – in efforts to reconstruct a functional left hand. Plastic surgery was still in its comparative infancy but I was lucky to have two young surgeons who had trained under Archibald McKindoe, the brilliant New Zealand born plastic surgeon who had revolutionised the treatment of severely injured World War Two RAF pilots. Clever Mr Golding and Mr Pulvertaft, through grafting surgery, sculpted my hand and manufactured a working thumb to give me an essential strong grip. It was made with a small spare bone from my elbow and skin taken from my lower abdomen, just above the pubic area. With this surgery I attained the dubious distinction of being one of few males in this world with a hairy left palm!

I missed huge chunks of school, which explains my having to later re-sit Maths 'O' Level five times. Fortunately I was already an avid reader and so other essential school subjects seemed not to be affected. However I did suffer endless teasing of the cruellest variety at my first primary school. 'Two Fingers Tim', was one typical taunt. My mother finally complained to the head teacher and I had to suffer the excruciating embarrassment of being hauled up onto the stage at a morning assembly.

"Tim Hughes has had a very bad accident with a lawn mower (sic)", said the headmaster, as he grabbed my arm and thrust my hand out to the shocked assembled kids. "He manages very well, and is no different to any of you". (Actually I had felt different for some time – as the sap was rising and inklings of gayness were coming to the surface.) "Anyone who teases him will be punished severely." The kids were spellbound and the warning did the trick. From then on I rarely experienced any torments from my schoolmates – save for one taunting bully later at Prep School, resulting in a very violent act of self-defence from me.

The only really serious discriminatory event occurred much later when I was in my last year in the grammar school Sixth

Form. I had applied for a Christmas holiday job at Selfridges – the huge department store on London's Oxford Street. The interview went well and I seemed to have landed the job, when suddenly the personnel manager noticed my hand as I was signing a form. He became flustered and said, "Oh dear, I see you have a deformed hand. I am afraid you won't be able to work here. Customers would be very put-off if you handled their purchases".

I fled in tears, as no one had ever accused me of deformity before. My father wrote an angry letter to the Selfridges chairman. We got a crawling apology offering me a job in the stockrooms. I did not take up the offer.

After the accident my parents lodged a liability suit against the College. They offered me a full scholarship to their very expensive posh institution. My parents felt that it might not be such a cool idea. They thought the background of the College's blame for an accident that occurred on their premises might cause resentment towards me. Instead after a legal hearing a judge awarded me the rather paltry damages of £800. They were invested by the court, on my behalf, in very low interest government gilt edged stocks – not accessible until I was twenty-one. It was a meagre amount even for those times. One can only imagine the value of such an award in today's climate of huge compensatory amounts.

I withdrew the full amount as soon as I was twenty-one. Because of volatile markets over a fourteen year period it was now worth well below the original sum. I blew it all on a Carnaby Street shopping spree, plus a leather motor-cycle jacket. It was the Swinging Sixties and I was already involved in the raunchy delights of the emerging Earls Court gay scene. Top of my list of hangouts was the Coleherne pub – the country's oldest fetish and 'leather boy' scene venue.

The Coleherne has always had a special place in my life. I discovered it when I was sixteen, and despite being underage managed to drink there and meet 'fellow travellers' with ease. I was adept at adding a few years to my real age, as I looked older, to avoid being dropped like the proverbial hot potato by prospective partners in crime. Yes, London may have been swinging, but despite the decriminalization recommendations of the 1957 Wolfenden Report, 'homosex' was a still severe crime – even more so if it involved a minor – and punishable by draconian prison sentences.

When later I won a scholarship to the London Academy of Music and Dramatic Art (LAMDA) – one of the UK's leading drama schools – right on the corner of Earls Court Road and Cromwell Road, and was living in the vicinity on Earls Terrace, it became my genuine local. But it had actually featured even earlier in my life.

When I was very small we lived close by the Coleherne in a flat on Redcliffe Square. My mother later told me that she would take us – my brother in a push chair – right passed the pub on our way for a regular afternoon walks in the Brompton Cemetery. She said that even then, in 1946, the clientele always looked very 'Bohemian'! The cemetery became one of the most notorious gay daytime 'cruising' areas during the sixties and seventies; with perhaps a glimpse of some blasphemous hottie, like the eponymous young man in the movie version of Joe Orton's *Entertaining Mr Sloane* doing press-ups on a grave.

Sadly the gay scene in Earls Court is no more. The clubs and pubs that catered for us have fallen victim to gentrification and exorbitant rents. The 'scene', both kinky and vanilla, has moved east to Soho and across the river to Vauxhall. In the more enlightened seventies and eighties, gay friendly pubs sprang-up in many London neighbourhoods. The Coleherne itself has become a ghastly up-market 'straight' gastro-pub.

3. Preparatory for Boys

Whitchurch House Preparatory School for Boys was located in the small village of the same name, across the ancient toll bridge spanning the Thames at Pangbourne, ten miles upstream from Reading. The school was in a large late Georgian house, with adjacent out-buildings. Its old stable block served as an art room and intimate theatre space. Art and dramatics were uniquely major parts of the curriculum – perfect for lad like me in the chrysalis stage of his gay development. In other ways it was a typical English prep boarding school of its times catering for sixty to seventy boys, from the ages of eight to thirteen – their purpose a stepping stone feeding a network of Public Schools.

The headmaster, Mr Davy, was a warm, charming and compassionate man – a perfect *in loco parentis* for young boys who had been wrenched from the normal embrace of family life. His very exotic wife, who looked like she might have stepped right out of Lawrence Durrell's novel, *The Alexandrian Quartet*, taught art and directed the school plays. By strange coincidence the young Larry Durrell, before he became the celebrated author, was the press officer to the British run government in Cyprus. He had been a frequent dinner guest at my parent's house in Famagusta after they left Egypt. I met him when visiting my parents in the summer holiday of 1955. His delightful *Bitter Lemons* is one of the best books on Cyprus. Naturally I soon became a big favourite of the headmaster's wife.

Mr Davy, an Oxford classics graduate, taught us Latin and Greek – required subjects then for entry to Public Schools. He was assisted by four more live-in male teachers who divvied up the subjects of English, Maths, History, French, History and Geography with varying degrees of expertise. The younger two teachers were also in charge of sport's activities. There was a visiting woman music specialist, and the local vicar came in to give us weekly religious instruction classes. Completing the staff was a cook, a gardener-cum-odd job man, a matron, and a very young and attractive assistant matron.

The assistant matron could not have been much older than eighteen and acted more like a big sister to us 'lost boys'. She had the unforgettably exotic name of Aurora and was naturally more popular with us than the rather dour much older Scots matron, Miss McKay. Especially when it was her turn to supervise us on bath nights. The boys bathed in twos sharing the water, cheekily flaunting our pubic parts at Aurora while she kept guard at the door. Hard to believe it but we only had a proper bath twice a week. Shower facilities were almost unheard of in those days; although there was a large eleven-seater sunken footbath in the basement changing room for communal wash-ups after sports' afternoons. We changed underwear and shirts twice a week and socks every two days – so different from our ultra-clean at any cost deodorant-driven present times. I can still recall that distinctly un-bathed, small boy rabbit-hutch like smell at night in the dormitories.

We soon discovered that Aurora was romantically involved with the Davy's son, an undergraduate at Oxford University. Someone had spied them snogging in the garden one afternoon. The rest of the staff were unmarried and during my time at the school only two of them appeared to have definite paedo-tendencies – somewhat below average for those times, at a boy's boarding school, I imagine.

The maths teacher cum football coach lived in a motor home permanently parked in the school grounds. Mr Reynolds, or Bummer Reg as we boys called him, used to invite the younger blond boys to his lair for what he euphemistically called 'private tuition'. Not being blond I was never invited – although I could definitely have benefited from extra maths tuition, having missed so many classes while I was in hospital. There was something obviously seedy about

Angelic Voices – me back row, second from right.

Bummer Reg – from his crumpled and stained suit, to his nicotine discoloured fingers. His breath smelled permanently of cigarettes. I was relieved never having to undergo the laying on of those particular hands, or heaven forbid, a kiss.

However Mr Haywood, the French and Geography master, who arrived in my second year at the school did show a special interest in me. He was a bachelor, like all the supporting staff, and had recently retired from the Royal Navy. He invariably wore a dark blue blazer with his old ship's insignia on the pocket patch. He must have been in his late forties, although I thought he seemed much older.

I often caught him staring at me – perhaps he recognised a kindred spirit in the making. I remember his particular delight when he made me up as Mme. Magloire, the Bishop's housekeeper, in our dramatization of the Jean Valjean candlestick stealing episode from *Les Miserable*. Like many keen schoolboy actors I always seemed to be cast in the female roles at school. Only once at that school did I play a male part. It was in a programme of scenes from Shakespeare, when my 'deformed' hand came in handy as I gave my pukka performance of a very evil Richard the Third. I also played Juliet in the famous balcony scene. It must have been quite a double act!

He never made an overt move on me at Whitchurch House, but swiftly placed all his bent cards on the table at my next school, Hill Place. During the Easter holidays in 1956, just as I was about to complete my last term before moving on to the Royal Grammar School in Colchester, my parents received a distressing letter from Mr. Davy. He had been 'forced to close the school down but every effort would be made to place boys at comparable other schools'. I was told later that his wife may have been medically induced to morphine dependence and that the alleged illicit provision of supplying her with opiates had caused them financial problems. It explained the day I had found a used syringe in the bathroom that the senior boy's dormitory shared with the head's family quarters.

I was devastated as it meant that I immediately lost touch with all my school friends. My parents chose to transfer me to Hill Place School in Maidstone. It was on Mr Davy's recommended list. Only two other boys – not close friends – ended up there with me. Mr Haywood was the lone member of Whitchurch House staff to transfer. I often wondered if he had been tipped off that his favourite boy would be waiting for him there.

In the long light evenings of that summer term Haywood would ask me to walk with him in the parkland beyond the school grounds under the pretext of preparing me for the Grammar School entrance exam. There was the usual initial grooming chat about girls. I quickly told him he was wasting his time as I liked boys. My candour made it easy for him to move on to the fondle moment and eventually to hands-on (his) masturbation. I enjoyed the attention and played along all through the term. I fear the reader may be coming all over moralistic at this point – but I would like to assure you, I always felt, even at this stage in my gay education, that I was equally a seducer and that I was really the one in control.

I learned that after I left Hill Place he tried it on with the wrong boy and was sacked after parental complaints. As was so often the case in those days he escaped prosecution – the parents in question were loath to subject their offspring to the traumatic ordeal of insensitive police enquiries, the resulting court case and inevitable *News of the World* front page story. Nowadays the media is choc-a-block with sympathetic historic tales of boarding school sexual abuse, but fortunately that purveyor of 'pedo' scandals and titillation, the Murdochian Sunday shocker tabloid, has no hand in the prurience as it bit the dust in 2010.

The only other male teacher at Whitchurch House was much younger. Only nineteen he had recently finished his 'A' levels at Wellington College and was waiting to take up a place at Trinity College, Dublin. He taught history and was a real star turn. A second generation White Russian his illustrious name was Nicholas Tolstoy (he later reverted to Nicolai). A member of a distinguished pre-Revolution aristocratic family, his father was a lawyer, and his grandfather

Whitchurch House Prep School.

had been the chamberlain to the last Tsar, Nicholas II. He was also distantly related to Leo Tolstoy, and in his later life, inaugurated the *War and Peace Balls*, which raised funds for White Russian charities.

He became famously embroiled in a lengthy notorious libel case in 1989, brought against him for his controversial writings about alleged British war crimes by a senior World War Two General in the British military. Eventually he became a big noise on the far right of the Conservative Party – jumping ship to UKIP in 1996 and standing as their candidate against the then Prime Minister, David Cameron, in

2010. He had lost his deposit at three previous elections as a Tory. Somewhere along the line he had inherited his father's title of Count Tolstoy.

We boys knew really nothing of his illustrious background, nor would have guessed about his future eminence on the Right. In those days he was just a charming, tall, and stunningly handsome young man. He was a huge favourite with the boys for his consummate talent as a storyteller. He regaled us at dormitory bedtimes with exciting readings of Conan Doyle's *Sherlock Holmes* and that same author's hero of the Napoleonic Wars, *Brigadier Gerard*. Other favourites were the colonial adventure yarns of Rider Haggard – *King Solomon's Mines* and *She*. His mother later married Patrick O'Brian, an enigmatic Irish writer, who became the international bestselling author of the Nelson period naval war stories – starting with *Master and Commander* in 1969. Exactly the kind of tales his stepson, Tolstoy, might have added to our dormitory reading list.

I don't remember a great deal of boy-on-boy hanky panky at Whitchurch House. There were the normal 'raging hormone' moments of furtive mutual masturbation, in the woods behind the school's vegetable garden, or in the swimming pool changing cabins. But nothing to match the exciting group 'circle jerks' I heard about from boarding school story-swaps later in my gay life. Returning to visit the school a few years ago I found that the big house had been broken up into flats; the gardens and playing fields had been thoroughly encroached on by a typical 1970s style private housing estate.

We had several very exotic foreign pupils; at least exotic to us English lads. They were boys from wealthy Indian and Iraqi families and they fascinated me. Memories perhaps of my earliest sexual adventure with Mohammed, our young Egyptian house boy. Many of the home grown boys were very prejudiced, admitting only that these 'foreigners' were 'rather good' on the cricket field. I, however, really enjoyed their company. They always seemed to have abundant pocket money and so perhaps it was just envy in those austere post-war days that fuelled the prejudice. Rather like Mohammed's gleaming set of golden dentistry they tended to flash around their expensive watches and bracelets and of course they all possessed that most prized item of those times – transistor radios.

One of the prettiest of these boys, Vihaan, would drag up in a sari and exotic make-up and with tinkling finger cymbals perform the most delicate of traditional Indian dances at our end of term concerts. Sensationally seductive and feminine when he danced he was in turn incredibly butch on the football and cricket fields.

I was particularly taken with Tewfik, a rather intense but handsome Iraqi boy. He was a year older than me and reminded me of Mohammed. But his skin was darker and although only thirteen he was very muscular and powerful looking. He used to swagger a lot and was something of a bully – a portent perhaps for his future role in life.

He quickly realised my crush and fostered a covert intimacy between us. We used to meet secretly in the sports changing room under the main house. He used to fuck me anally, or 'bum' me, as we used to call it. It was my first experience of this kind of sex and not something that I really enjoyed then, or even after in 'the life'. It was mainly due to a very violent act on Tewfik's part. One day he carved a piece of wood in the shape of a rudimentary cock and tried to rape me with it.

I bled for a day but I was far too scared to go to matron for help. Fortunately it must have been a superficial wound and despite some extreme soreness it healed quite quickly. Years later I was not really surprised when I saw Tewfik again – this time in an entirely appropriate setting. I was watching a news story about Baghdad, just prior to the US/British invasion of

Iraq in 2003. He was sitting at a table to the right hand of Saddam Hussein and was obviously a senior member of his inner ruling Sunni cabinet circle. After the fall of Saddam he was imprisoned and finally publicly executed.

The only other act of violence at the school was instigated by a boy who continually teased and bullied me about my hand. One day I could no longer tolerate his taunts and snapped. I picked up a metal roller skate and slashed him across the face. There was lots of blood and he was rushed to the hospital in Reading to be stitched – he probably bears a scar to this day. I was never bothered by him again and when Mr Davy found out that I had been provoked I was not punished.

My best friend there was Dudley Davenport. A fellow drama buff, he played the convict, Valjean, in *The Bishop's Candlesticks*. He lived in London – just off Gloucester Road, in a huge mansion flat in Harrington Gardens. He invited me to stay one half-term holiday. A very welcome treat, as I was still sequestered at Nan's house in Winchester during school holidays. His divorced mum was Canadian and very bohemian, to my young eyes. She was the person that first introduced me to Birds Eye Frozen Peas. She also took us to see my first West End show – the very popular long-running English musical by Julian Slade, *Salad Days*.

Years later, when I was a student at LAMDA, I had a secret affair with an Old Vic company actor called David Dodimead. His agent, Elspeth Cochrane, was responsible for getting me my first theatre job at the Ipswich Arts Theatre. His actual long term partner, James Cairncross, had been one of the original leading cast members of *Salad Days*. I purloined his witty Night Club Manager's song from the show, 'Cleopatra', for musical auditions with great success.

The other noteworthy thing about staying with Dudley Davenport was my discovery of a notorious 'cruisy' gent's toilet at Gloucester Road Tube Station. It would prove especially significant when I was seventeen as the location where I was picked up by a very famous movie star.

4. Grammar School Days

Rare indeed are the moments when one realises the relentless movement of time. That moment comes most acutely, when an event suddenly brings one vividly in touch with one's own past. One of these moments came to me when I returned recently to the Grammar School for the opening of a new theatre space – built in honour of the teacher, George Young, who mentored my early thespian days. On Colchester's North Hill, in the bus from the railway station, I saw a swarm of boys in purple blazers; my eyes turned inwards and I was immediately looking back across the vast distance of the past – across a space of almost sixty years.

That was when a station porter had loaded my trunk and suitcase into a taxi and with my beloved Mum in tow, a thirteen year old boy in brand new purple blazer was carried up that hill and around into Lexden Road to his new school: Colchester Royal Grammar School (CRGS). Ahead were some of the happiest days of my life. Six years to find the appropriate dancing shoes, before I hoofed it on to those cities of utmost gaiety – Swinging Sixties London and in the 1970s, 'The City That Never Sleeps', New York.

In truth initially I was not so happy. This new school was much bigger and somewhat alien to me after Whitchurch House. My first term there was difficult. I am ashamed to say I even ran away. Slipping out of the boarding house after breakfast one morning, I took three changes of bus across Essex to my parent's house near Saffron Walden. My father had recently returned from Cyprus and was the CO at RAF Debden. I arrived at the house and feeling immensely foolish had to hide in the shrubbery for almost two hours, as my mother was hosting an officer's wives coffee morning.

My parents telephoned the housemaster, Mr Donson, and a chastened new boy was driven back to the school. I was not punished – the headmaster was never informed, and the whole thing was hushed up. After that barmy event, the housemaster and his wife were extra kind towards me. I began eventually to make good and lasting friendships and settled down to six crammed years of academics, theatrics and the discovery of my brand new world of gaiety.

CRGS had been founded as a town grammar school in the thirteenth century for the poor scholar sons of burghers and local tradesmen. It subsequently received two royal charters – from Henry VIII in 1539 and Elizabeth I in 1584. So it became doubly, a Royal Grammar School – with hideous purple blazers emblazoned with three gold crowns on pocket patches that marked one out for agro from the town 'oiks'.

Somewhere along the line it began to ape the great nine nineteenth century Victorian public schools and absorb the ethos and style of Dr Arnold's transformation of Rugby School. By the beginning of the twentieth century it was almost indistinguishable from them. It had gained a house system, boarders, gold lettered rolls of university honours in the assembly hall, a feeder preparatory school (closed by my time), and an old boy's society called the Old Colcestrians. It also played rugby, that eponymous gentlemen's game – rather than soccer the sport of 'oiks'. It only differed from the public school system in that it was funded by the state through the Essex County Education Authority, instead of by parental fees. After the war, its admission policy was the dreaded 11-plus exam – an unkind lottery introduced by the Atlee Labour government, in place of the public schools, Common (sic) Entrance Exam.

The only real difference from the public schools, at least during my time there, was a seeming complete absence of teacher/boy abuse in the time honoured boarding-school tradition. Maybe this was because CRGS was essentially a day school with only a small number of boarders. We were overseen by a very family orientated housemaster, Jim Donson and his

CRGS – School House and the Library.

ex-nurse wife, Marjorie, who acted as matron. They had two young daughters who treated us boys almost like big brothers. It was rather like we were a kind of extended family.

There were only two members of staff who were assumed to be queer – Mr Hall, a science master and Mr Billet (Dirty Bill) a French teacher. They shared a house several streets away from the school, in a discreet relationship typical of homosexual couples of that time. Billet was fond of calling the prettiest boys to his desk at the front of the classroom when he was marking their homework. The urban legend was that the further you let him run his hand up your short-trousered leg the more marks you got. I never heard of anything more overtly paedophile than this – certainly none of the 'grooming' stories, leading to sexual abuse, one reads about in historic boarding school cases before the courts to-day. This was somewhat disappointing to a 'gayboy' like me, who definitely would have appreciated some adult male attention. Perhaps it contributed to my quest for older male experiences outside the school.

Schools were very different then – nothing like today's mod cons, with computer work stations and countless other electronic gizmos. The only modern teaching tool was a sixteen millimetre film projector, jealously guarded by the geography teacher, Gob Fancourt. He was named Gob because he rained down projectiles of spit on his classes while manning the projector. We were even forbidden to use biros and fountain pens loaded with an ink cartridge were *de rigueur*. Each subject had a core set syllabus and it was like rote learning.

Discipline was far more rigid. Corporal punishment was still legal, although caning was used very sparingly at CRGS. I do remember some occasional mass slipperings on our pyjama covered bums for the crime of talking after lights-out, by a sadistic new young assistant housemaster.

The headmaster, Jack Elam, was a lovely cultured gentleman who must have been responsible for the comparative absence of cruelty and the relaxed regimen of discipline at the school. He had a green-fingered wife who oversaw the splendid gardens the school was set in. In fact, it was she that cultivated the horticultural bug in the young but later celebrated RHS gardener, Beth Chatto, the sister of my friend and mentor, Seley Little. He was the gay local paper drama critic.

They had three teenage children, Nick, Jane and Caroline. Nick was already in the Sixth form when I arrived at the school and after Oxford he went on to a distinguished career in the diplomatic corps, eventually becoming Ambassador to Luxemburg. Caroline attended the Girl's High School and became a lasting friend. As with the Donsons, we were treated almost like members of the headmaster's extended family.

Caroline was almost a contemporary. She was a budding actress and played Juliet in one of my early directing attempts, an open air production of *Romeo and Juliet*. At a fund raising performance for a charity then called, The Spastic Society. She was almost immolated *a la* Brunnhilde in Wagner's

Gotterdammerung, along with a group of very disabled spastics (that was the term then, sadly) in the audience front row. An over enthusiastic stage-manager had overdone the lighter fluid in the flaming torches carried by Paris and his servant in the tomb scene.

After Oxford she did a post-graduate art history degree at the Courtauld Institute, and was in the same year there as Paul Lewis, a best chum from my other teen world, the school holiday courses at the British Drama League. Yet another of those interconnected 'six degrees of separation' friendships that seem to permeate my life. They both went on to hold lecturing posts at universities and Caroline then became the editor of *The Burlington Magazine.*

Jack Elam must have been a very perceptive man. After all, he gave me Dudley, our gay bishop and chairman of the school governors to look after on that fateful Sports Day in 1959. On one occasion the art master, Johnny Graham, saw me in town sitting in the passenger seat of the notorious local gay artist Denis Wirth-Miller's car, stopped at the traffic lights. He tried unsuccessfully to drag me out of the car and then reported me to the headmaster. Jack Elam's relaxed reaction and judgement on the incident perfectly displayed itself in his immortal words, "I think Hughes knows what he is doing".

Hughes certainly did. I was approaching my eighteenth birthday party where the party's guest list would include Panorama's Robert Kee and TV personality, Daniel Farson. I had had a sexual encounter with Britain's movie-star heartthrob, Dirk Bogarde, and was hobnobbing in wickedest Soho with the country's most famous queer painter, Francis Bacon.

Public opinion on homosexuality may have changed significantly since my time at school. Many secondary schools in the country now actually have a Gay Society, along with the beloved Stamp Clubs and Debating Societies of my time. I never felt any sense of real discrimination, or danger; although

Dirk Bogarde – a 'Cottage' Encounter.

occasionally I was teased and called a 'pouf'. Neither did I
experience any bullying. I think this was because at CRGS,
prowess on the rugby field was no more important than
academic achievement, or appreciation of artistic excellence –
the annual school play, in which I always excelled, was indeed
one of the highlights of the school calendar. Later I met many
gays whose own schooldays were intolerable, all because of their
perceived 'otherness'. So perhaps I was just lucky.

5. School Friends and other Partners in Crime

I had a sprinkling of sexual trysts with boys around my own age but these were mostly of the 'hormone raging' exploratory kind, centred on mutual masturbation – typical in an all male boarding school environment. I often fancied dayboys at the school but these boys were mostly unavailable. In any case, dayboys were well able to direct these adolescent 'urges' in a perfectly hetero manner towards pupils at the local Colchester High School for Girls. As a matter of fact at least three of my school friends dated and eventually married their teenage sweethearts from the High School. The few dayboys I had a real crush on I would invite, with wicked intent, to visit me at my parent's, or grandmother's house, during half-term holidays.

There were to my knowledge only four boys – Alan, Brian, John and David – who on leaving school went on to identify as gay. That's not counting Mike, the predatory senior boy manager of Tuck Shop fame and another handsome, super-athletic senior boy called Toby. I only found out about Toby when I often found him, many years later, in the popular gay 'cruisy' toilet at Baker Street Tube station close to my London flat.

His brother, Ralph, who was an exact contemporary dayboy friend of mine, eventually shared a room with me at the London University hostel behind Harrods during my first term at LAMDA. He was as attractive as his elder brother but definitely not of the gay persuasion. The only time we ever shared any kind of intimacy was when one night during the frightening days of the Cuban Missile crisis, we clung together in bed listening to a transistor radio, not sure if we would survive until morning as it seemed the end of the world was almost certainly nigh.

Alan Wilcox was a dayboy. We shared a desk in the third form and during my first year at the school became best friends. His mother, hearing about the sorry quality of boarding house food, took pity on me and would pack extra sandwiches for us to share at lunchtime. He was initially profoundly guilty about his emerging gayness and seriously considered a life of celibacy. When he left school at sixteen he fled his not very understanding parent's home in Brightlingsea to sort himself out in London. After an unhappy stint as a clerk with an insurance company, he decided on celibacy and entered a Catholic seminary in Yorkshire.

I lost touch with him for a several years, but just before leaving for New York ran into him on Earls Court Tube station, now proudly gay and in the company of Ian, his partner. They have remained together for over fifty years – became civil partners in 2004 and are now married. I would often visit them at their flat just off Leicester Square. It had been a rented council flat which they bought in the sale-off bounty of the Thatcher era. They are now sitting on a property worth a small fortune. Sadly, Alan is now in the advanced stages of dementia but fortunately has the perfect carer.

Brian Ashen was a boarder in the year below me. He was a gifted actor and joined the British Drama League youth group with me in the school holidays. We shared a flat for several years, just off Baker Street, when I was teaching drama at Tulse Hill Comprehensive Boy's School, before I left for New York. He worked as a continuity announcer and news reader for the BBC World Service. Brian was an inveterate world traveller and seemed to have a hot boyfriend in every port of call. This included Tyrone, a young black guy he had met when he came to see me in New York. When Tyrone became ill with the 'gay plague' in 1984, and was unable to get health insurance to cover his hospitalizations, he moved to live with Brian in London. He died a few months later at the Mile End Hospital. Brian took his ashes back to his family in South Carolina. In typical Brian fashion he perched a glass of Tyrone's favourite red wine next to the ashes in the aircraft's overhead luggage bin for the flight back to Charlotte.

Janusz, a stunningly beautiful Polish lad, with jet black hair and piercing blue eyes, was my favourite of Brian's boys. Although he was not an actor Derek Jarman had plucked him from the street to play one of the gay centurions in his first film, *Sebastiane*. Brian leant me his sonorous BBC trained voice – he had already majestically played God, in Benjamin Britten's *Noye's Fludde*, during his last year at CRGS – as narrator for my radio production of Stravinsky's *The Soldier's Tale*. We recorded it in the BBC Maida Vale Studios in 1970, with a young cast of my ex-Tulse Hill pupils. By this time I had returned to college to get a teaching certificate.

John Gibbs was two years above me in the boarding house and we were not particularly close. When he left the school he became a successful advertising account manger in the *Mad Men* mode of those times. I had lost touch with him. Then by a fortuitous accident in my first year at LAMDA he became one of my best London friends. Late one night I was cruising the darkened toilet – there was a special breed of 'cottagers' whose helpful community service was to remove light bulbs – on the emergency staircase at Lancaster Gate Tube Station. I bumped into him there. He introduced me to a horny world of young black American servicemen marooned far from their Stateside homes, escaping their Suffolk airbases for a weekend of gay adventures in London. We provided parties and sex, they supplied tax free ciggies and booze from the PX store on their base.

John already had a set of creative trend-setting gay Swinging Sixties friends who soon became my friends as well. Notably Nigel Quiney – the brilliant designer of iconic 60s gift-wrap, that folks were literally buying-up in rolls to use as trendy wallpaper. It was even rumoured that Princess Margaret and Lord Snowdon had used it in one of their Kensington Palace toilets. Nigel was also the host of some of the best parties I had ever been to, held in his eerie of a flat overlooking the railway tracks at West Hampstead. Just as importantly he introduced me to the delights and dangers of night-time cruising on Hampstead Heath.

Also through John I met the Welsh songwriter Gil King and his jewellery designer black boyfriend, Carlton Payne. I frequently used the very sexy Carlton as a photo shoot model when I became an editor in the late 1960s at *Jeremy*, Britain's first gay magazine. Gil was the personal assistant to Kenneth Hume, Shirley Bassey's rent boy loving bisexual husband and agent. Then there was John's flatmate, Richard Perfitt, a BBC film editor, whose Mum sent him to a psychiatrist to cure him unsuccessfully from gaiety. And lastly David Nutter, brother to Tommy, the Saville Row tailor who was all the rage at that time. David was the in-house photographer to John Lennon and Yoko Ono, and later after John's murder to Elton John.

In the Seventies, when we had both moved to New York, David took me several times with Lennon and his 'secret' Japanese mistress, May Pang, to Kellers, the gay waterfront bar at the foot of Christopher Street. It had the best Blues juke box in town and Lennon would feed it with quarters for hours. This was also the bar where I first met my East Village neighbour and running buddy, Robert Mapplethorpe. By day, in the early 1970s, Keller's was a transvestite pick-up bar for butch straight truckers in *The Last Exit to Brooklyn* mould whose trucks were parked at night by the piers. Gay men used them for sex late at night, as portrayed in the Al Pacino gay serial killer movie, *Cruising*. By night Kellers magically transformed itself into New York's first leather bar and as a cruising venue for 'dinge queens' – gay men with a predilection for young 'trade' of colour.

It was truly a virtual 'outlaw' paradise – the natural progression for someone whose 'rebel' initiation had been made in those far off Grammar School nights, at Colchester's Headgate Pub. It was there I had my first encounters with the 'queer' underworld of the 1950s. The pub was even managed by a man with the apt name of Mr Lawless.

John Gibbs came to live in Nottingham Place with Brian and me for a short time, while he was searching for a new flat. We inherited all the fashionable stripped-pine kitchen furniture from his old flat in Paddington. I always stayed with him in his new Goldhawk Road flat, whenever I came back to visit London from New York.

David Perry was three years younger, and like myself more

Bow ties were all the rage then!

aware and accepting of his gayness from a very early age. He was also a talented actor. He played the Porter to my Macbeth and I directed him in several productions, notably as Capulet, in *Romeo and Juliet*. Like his best friend at school, Jim Acheson, he went on to a career in the world of theatre and film costume design.

He left the Grammar School at sixteen and enrolled at the Colchester School of Art, where he was noted for his tap dancing ,over the top gayness and the staging of zany camp

41

theatrical revues. After college he became the wardrobe manager at the Royal Shakespeare Company in Stratford. I was not thrilled when he poached my valuable young wardrobe mistress find when I was assistant manger at the Ipswich Arts Theatre. But us gay Old Colcestrians needed to stay together, so I soon forgave him.

In 1970 he was offered the same position at the Tyrone Gutherie inspired Shakespeare Theatre in Stratford Ontario, Canada. I used to fly up from New York and we would cruise the gay bathhouses and leather bars of Toronto and Detroit together. Those cities were remarkably almost an equidistant 120 miles night-drive from Stratford. Our favourite was The Library, a quirky Toronto bathhouse with a study room copiously furnished with shelves of unread books and writing desks. I am certain its patrons did most of their close study in the steam room.

Brian, John and David were, unlike myself and Alan, very sporty and all accomplished 'rugger-bugger' members of the various school rugby fifteens. There was no way they could be considered 'sissies', although David could be marvellously 'camp', something of a novelty in those austere 50s times. Sadly they all succumbed as early British casualties to AIDS – the plague then raging through our gay world. Despite my frequent early warnings from New York, unknowingly they had contracted HIV in the early 1980s. Brian and John died in 1989 and David in 1992. By the time of their deaths I had already lost many friends and the two most important people in my life to the disease. That was when I discovered that the big un-gay part of this gay life is being a lone survivor.

I write these words as I approach my seventy-six birthday. A time one imagined one might have had heaps of old gay friends still. Thank goodness then for those straight good friends from the Grammar School – particularly Jim Acheson and Nicholas Heightman, a special friend, who went on to Loughborough

Right at the centre of New York's Gay Village!

University and then to work in pharmacology. Bizarrely in the early 1990s, in yet another 'six degrees of separation' moment in my life, he pitched up as the Burroughs-Wellcome pharma rep for AZT, the first HIV anti-retroviral drug, at Beth Israel Medical Center. This was the very hospital where I was then working as a social worker in their HIV program.

When I was seventeen I had an enormous crush on Jim. He was one of the dayboys I took to my Nan's in Winchester during a half-term. Thank goodness he rebuffed my attempt at seduction and that it just became a wicked episode to scandalously regale our friends with in later years. Amazingly, despite his 'straightness' he has become celebrated in one the gayest of all careers – movie costume design – with three Oscars to his name.

His parents, entirely ignorant of my predatory intent, welcomed me into their house. I always like to think I was able to help counter their typical parental resistance to his rarefied career choice and his desire to prepare for it by getting a place at art school. I remember his father saying that such a choice would almost certainly lead to a life of penury.

In fact no sooner had he left art school than he was working at the BBC, where among other productions he cut his teeth designing early episodes of *Doctor Who*. He has designed the costumes and sometimes the entire production design for over thirty-two major European and Hollywood films. He created the costumes for the first three original blockbuster *Spiderman* movies, that by way of several films with the Monty Python team, three films for Bernardo Bertolucci – *The Last Emperor*, *The Sheltering Sky* and *Little Buddha* – and Stephen Frears' sensational, *Dangerous Liaisons*.

I doubt that he has ever been 'a starving artist' but regrettably neither his father, nor his mum lived to see their very talented and famous son's enormous success.

There was another much older dayboy I had a serious unrequited crush on. I don't believe he has ever been aware of my feelings. John Sutherland, four or five years my senior, was in his last years in the Sixth Form. I got to know him when I made my drama debut at the Grammar School. I was a member of the rabble forum crowd in *Julius Caesar*, but also had the small speaking part of servant to Brutus. John was a superb Brutus. There was something very 'outlaw' about him, compared to his Sixth Form contemporaries. He had a severe, almost crewcut hairstyle, and frequented those 'all the rage' venues of the 1950s – coffee bars and the local jazz club.

He lived with grandparents but his mother had a flat in the same house as my artist friend Joe Robinson's basement home. She seemed drop dead glamorous to my 'hetero' innocent young eyes. Through Joe's front window, as I lay on his divan of a Sunday, I had an almost 'up-skirting' view of her descending the steps always in alluring high heels and sexy nylon stockings.

In yet one more of those 'six degrees of separation' coincidences in my life, I discovered that my best friend at teacher's training college, Hugh Watt, had a sister and she was married to John Sutherland. They had met when she was a student and John was a young lecturer in the English department at Edinburgh University. He later went on to a distinguished career as a *Guardian* columnist, author of many books of criticism and literary biography and as a professor at University College London (UCL). John is retired from teaching now but remains the Emeritus Nothcliffe Professor of Modern English Literature at UCL.

He has also written a fascinating memoir, *The Boy Who Loved Books*, that contains sections of his time as a pupil at the Grammar School. It is a very different take on life at the school than is mine, and displays a condemnation of the place and degree of personal unhappiness that I feel has much to do with his somewhat dislocated family upbringing. I think, judging by his obvious affection for life as an army recruit doing his National Service, he would have been much happier as a boarder.

He has recently co-authored a book with his adopted gay son, Jack, who was at different times in Hollywood, the bodyguard to the outrageous black drag queen and television personality, RuPaul, movie actor Mickey Rourke and the rockband REM's Michael Stipe. It describes vividly a life of growing up in an 'outlaw' style that in some ways matches his Dad's Colchester life – but this time it is Southern California, where John taught for many semesters at the California Institute of Technology in Pasadena. *Stars, Cars and Crystal Meth* is, I think, one of the modern classics of addiction and recovery and fully compliments Sutherland's memoir of his own addiction and move to sobriety, *Last Drink to LA*.

Once again, in another of my 'six degrees of separation' moments, RuPaul happens to be best buddies and a protégé of that iconic New York nineties drag-queen and gay activist friend of mine, The Lady Bunny!

The grammar school is a very different place to-day. It is always represented at the top of the country's league tables for passes in the 'A' level examination and university places. Girls are now admitted to the Sixth Form but the boarding house is now only available to fee paying Sixth Formers. When I Googled the school recently I was surprised to see it was renown for its success in inter-school championship games of Ping-Pong. This was all explained when I discovered that the majority of Sixth Formers were from China. More worrying to me is that it has now become, through the misguided education provisions of the present Tory government, that most dreaded type of all twenty-first century scholastic institutions – an Academy.

I wonder how it shapes up in the present day diversity stakes? When I was at the school there were no boys of colour and the only circumcised lad was Jewish. I do know this, however, when I wrote to the school in the 1990s, suggesting that a group of old boys would like to commission and fund a memorial stain glass window to commemorate our three contemporaries who had fallen to the gay plague, I never even received a reply.

6. Love Amongst the Doughnuts

The school tuck shop was overseen by a master who taught Latin. We called him 'The Baron'. Short and stout, with a swagger to compensate for his height, he was a barrel-chested brute with a military-crop haircut. He could be particularly harsh towards boys who did not play the game – and that game was rugby. He was the head coach for the First Fifteen, staffing the tuck shop with his team favorites. Scathing of anyone he deemed 'a pansy' – the popular derisory term then for a slightly 'sissyboy' like me – he would have been mortified to learn that several of his hand picked 'rugger-buggers' were just that – buggers!

Sex between boys was quite rare among the dayboys but in the boarding house after lights out, when hormones must have been at their most raging, it was a different story. And while it was definitely a fleeting phase for most, a small subset of my closest pals went on to be fully paid up members of 'The Gay Life' when they left school. Three of them were stalwart members of the rugby teams and in no way sissy. Much later in the 1980s, all three were among the UK's earliest AIDS casualties.

I had warned my Old Colcestrian friends, in letters and on my visits back to London, about the horrible disease that was scything its way through the gay communities of New York and San Francisco. Tragically with the virus's long incubation period to full blown AIDS, I must have been too late.

The tuck shop at CRGS was a small padlocked wooden hut at one side of our playground, set against the swimming pool walls. It had hatched windows that opened up to serve unhealthy but tasty sweet-tooth confections to us boys, weaned on the boring but healthy comparatively sugar-free wartime rationing. Wagon Wheels and Penguin Biscuits were big favorites, but pride of place went to the doughnut. Three trays of these sugary jam-filled delights, were delivered fresh from a local bakery every morning.

The tuck shop was open at lunch times and during the mid-morning milk break. Labour's post-war Clement Atlee government's 'freebie' third of a pint of milk was on offer for secondary as well as primary school pupils still. This was long before the Edward Heath Tory government's Education Minister became notorious as 'Maggie Thatcher Milk Snatcher', and the little bottles were then banished even from junior school playgrounds; secondary school bottles had already been snatched earlier. Later she paid the price when Oxford University refused to grant her an honorary degree.

When closed the tuck shop became the site of illicit card game gambling. Even less licit was its use by one strapping First Fifteen member for clandestine schoolboy 'sexcapades'. Mike, like me, was an army-brat boarder. His father was stationed in Aden and at the time he was in the Remove, an aptly named weigh-station between the Fifth and Sixth forms, that warehoused less academic boys who were ineligible for the Sixth form. Sequestered there, they sat and re-sat GCE 'O' Levels until they qualified for the Sixth, or marked time until National Service beckoned.

Compulsory military service for males of eighteen was mandatory from the end of the war right up to the year before I left school. Although in its last few years, with a fast disappearing British Empire no longer in need of protection, it was easy to get deferments – especially if you pretended to be 'queer'. So being gay did have one positive aspect.

Mike was a trusted Baron favorite. He held a tuck shop key and was in charge of the doughnuts. These he dispensed gratis, using a predatory 'servicing' tariff to younger boys in thrall to his craggy glamour and fame on the rugby field. He was what I would call in later life – 'a bona butch brute'.

A simple 'suck-off' would get you one doughnut while the

Jam-filled delights in exchange for sexual favours.

full works, a 'bumming', got you a well earned two of those sugary prizes. Bring along a tag-team buddy and you would hit the jackpot – a whole three jammy delicacies to share. So that dear reader is how, at the not so tender age of thirteen, I found myself naked in the tuck shop.

As for poor predatory, Mike? Charmed as he was during his schooldays he came to the kind of end we might call as sticky as the doughnuts. After National Service in the Royal Navy he joined the Hong Kong river police. Some time later in the mid 1970s he was brutally murdered, either by a criminal gang, perhaps the dreaded 'Tongs', or possibly a sexploited young partner. The whole thing bore an uncanny resemblance to the fate of the closeted character Merrick, portrayed in the very different Indian colonial setting as part of the plot of the popular book and 1984 TV mini-series, *The Jewel in the Crown*. Mike was found early one morning with his throat cut floating in Hong Kong's scenic harbour.

7. Cottages – the Original Gay Social Network

Jumbo is the gigantic water tower that bestrides Balkerne Gate instantly visible as you approach Colchester station by train. You can't miss it. It was erected in 1893; the largest one ever built by the Victorians, gaining its nickname from the enormous elephant that had recently arrived at London Zoo. It still stands proud after more than a century but now well past its use, while sadly all those other water 'conveniences' from the Victorian era have long disappeared from Colchester and everywhere throughout the land.

The late Victorian 'Spend a penny brigade' decreed that 'public conveniences' be built throughout the kingdom. Colchester's local burghers of that time had seen to it that their town was well endowed with these municipal marvels. In our contemporary Britain, starved of public toilets, it is easy to forget their ubiquity on the cityscape and how they gradually evolved to serve a dual purpose – thanks to the pioneering ingenuity of a clandestine gay community. Long before the pornucopia of gay pubs and clubs, discos, online cruising, and its raunchy ancestors the phone-sex lines and personal newspaper ads – the 'cottage', as they came to be known, was literally the only game in town.

They came in all shapes and sizes. Gigantic subterranean ones – like the fabulously tiled fantasy beneath St Pancras Station with its ceramic rotunda urinals filling the grand space like some *Come Dancing* formation routine, and forever known by us cruising aficionados as the Haunted Ballroom. There were stinky narrow little 'hole in the wall' kinds, often with fag-end blocked gullys overflowing with old urine; the ornate wrought iron French style 'pissoir' species like those on the Thames Embankment in Chelsea. All across London there were the under-the-street breed with gleaming glass cisterns encased in polished brass. Outside the cities we had the smelly variety, cement block bunkers in lay-bys alongside major roadways. But everywhere, throughout the entire land, they were in the archetypal rustic cottage-type style that first appeared in Edwardian times, and that gave their gay slang name to the pursuit of 'cottaging'.

It must have been when I was in the third form at CRGS, and just about fourteen, that I stumbled on that essential key to provincial gay life – the 'cottage'. Their very existence was a godsend to a curious gay lad in the nineteen-fifties, eager for sexual experience but as yet too underage to seek it in seedy pubs, or the 'queer' private members drinking clubs that had secretly emerged in London and a few larger cities since the war. All my early important gay friendships, and my initiation into that life, flow from those early adventures in 'cottaging'.

Sunday afternoons – mornings meant mandatory church attendance – were unsupervised in the boarding house. After lunch we were free to do whatever we liked. For me, after a first eye-opening initial experience in Castle Park, it became prime 'cottaging' time. The park sloped down to the River Colne behind the historic keep. All that's left of the castle built by William the Conqueror on the foundations of a Roman temple to Claudius. There were three toilets in the park. The 'no-go' cruising one (too many straight patrons) at the entrance gates, next to the Georgian Hollytrees Museum, and then two more of the more rustic cottage variety within the park itself. It was in one of these one afternoon, while sitting on a bench, that I became aware of a steady stream of lingering convenience users. Instantly intrigued I investigated and was soon a regular participant on that scene. A scene that might involve mutual masturbation; sometimes fellatio; rarely anal intercourse and on odd occasions an invitation to go home to someone's house.

It amazes me that I was never caught by the cops – in this country anyway. [I was, however, arrested in Lafayette Park opposite the White House, when I was visiting my parents in Washington, during the Christmas holidays of 1961. I had foolishly mistaken the local cruising protocols.] Especially as police surveillance and entrapment was very common in those days. For the police, 'queer patrol' provided an easy collar. If you were unlucky enough to be caught, you might be charged with 'soliciting for an immoral purpose', 'public indecency', or most serious of all – 'sodomy'. Some police forces notoriously used cute young cadets as decoy bait to tempt us 'poufs' into behaving recklessly.

A court appearance could ruin a man's career. It could also destroy family life, as many 'cottagers' were in fact married men moonlighting in our twilight world. There were draconian punishments in the form of large fines, long prison sentences, and always a very public shaming in the pages of your local paper. You could even be charged with these same offences if the acts took place not in a toilet, but in the privacy of your own home.

In the local paper it might be buried on the inside pages if you were not a person in the public eye – a lowly postman, office worker, or bank clerk; but it would be front page ruin for a member of the clergy, or a teacher – especially if it involved choir boys, or pupils under your care. Most scandalous during my time at the school was the cottage arrest of a prominent Conservative member of the town council, who the year before had been Mayor of Colchester. He got the full treatment in the *News of the World*. It was a fate that befell several well known members of the establishment at that time.

The most infamous case of all involved Lord Montagu of Beaulieu, the founder of the vintage car museum in the New Forest. This 1954 case was the most sensational 'gross indecency' legal action since Oscar Wilde's and it led to prison sentences for Montagu and two other men, Peter Wildeblood and William Pitt Rivers, scion of the family that gave us the wonderful Oxford anthropology museum. Wildeblood was a *Daily Mail* journalist and from his prison experience bravely wrote, *Against the Law*, a pioneering book that was the prime impetus for setting up Parliament's Wolfendon Report – and in 1967, the eventual decriminalization of certain homosexual acts. Montague's name even entered schoolboy slang of the time, as in 'to Monty', or 'Montague' someone – meaning the act of anal intercourse!

'Cottaging' could be sometimes scary – one was easy prey for feral gangs of teenage 'queer bashers'. But at other times it could be very amusing. The cottage was after all a great leveller, catering to gays from all walks of life. At CRGS, sometime after my Castle Park initiation, it provided me with two important gay relationships – friendships with men that led to an education and experiences unavailable to the average provincial gay teenager of that time.

I soon learned to lie about my age in cottage encounters. After all it was not until 1999 that the consensual male age was lowered to sixteen. I always thought it was desperately unfair that girls of my age could have sex with impunity! But back then it was illegal even if you were collecting your old age pension. Not that it dissuaded the senior citizens I sometimes met. Once in the Castle Park loo I was wooed by an old man with dentures. He insisted on showing me his party trick by taking them out and arranging them tiara style on his folded three corner shaped handkerchief on the top of his very bald head, announced he was Queen Victoria and was having, "a lovely Jubilee!"

One particular funny scene occurred when I was sitting in a toilet cubicle in an Uxbridge park. I suddenly became aware of a guy brandishing a Black & Decker hand drill, peering over the wall from the next cubicle. "Can I plug this into your light socket, mate", he requested, "mine's not working!" I said he could but quickly pulled up my pants and exited to the blissful sound of yet another 'glory hole' being drilled.

I soon learned the etiquette of cubicle cruising. This might include toe tapping in the gap under adjoining cubicle walls; sexy preferences scribbled on the harsh toilet paper of that time,

A subterranean 'gents', circa 1960s.

slipped under those walls; or for the very daring, kneeling down and copping a genital feel. Apocryphal I am sure, but hilarious never the less, the cottage legend of a man passing a note under to ask about his neighbour's preferred sex acts and getting back the reply, "Arresting people – please step outside, sir."

After the Castle Park, the busiest loos were the ones next to the 'flea-pit' cinema close to St Botolph's Priory, another in the Culver Street car park opposite the public library, useful for bookish types like me, and the one behind the Headgate pub – always with the ubiquitous missing light bulbs.

The jewel in the crown of the Colchester cruising scene was the lorry drivers' hangout at the bottom of North Hill, on the by-pass roundabout. It had the most amazingly obscene *grafitti* I had ever seen and included a whole series of scrawled personal want sex ads – it was surely the proto-type for the internet's gay social networks.

It was one fateful encounter in this particular toilet that gave me entry to a *demi-monde* of artists, media personalities, lawyers, Harley Street eye specialists, and even peers of the realm. It was a gay world I could only have dreamed about.

That fateful cottage encounter when I was seventeen was meeting Denis Wirth-Miller. He was a locally notorious 'queer' artist. Denis was a member of Wivenhoe's notable post-war bohemian set and best friend to the much more famous painter of that time, Francis Bacon. Bacon also bought a house there so he could be close to his good pals. Denis's boyfriend was the James Bond cover illustrator and Royal College of Art teacher, Richard (Dickie) Chopping. Wivenhoe was an old fishing port, on that same river that ran through Castle Park.

Denis picked me up and whisked me away to the home that he shared with Dickie. It was a converted old warehouse on the quayside. They had called it the Storehouse when they bought it just after the war. Dickie must have been away at their *pied a terre* flat in London that night. From that evening there followed almost two years of Denis's courtship as he introduced me to a glittering gay circle of the rich and sometimes famous.

I had heard all about him, with suitable dire warnings, from my friend another local artist, Joseph Robinson. Joe was the first important mentor I had met in one of those Castle Park 'cottages' some two years before. He really was the archetypal 'struggling artist' who supported his painting by making a meagre living framing and restoring paintings. Joe, more than anyone, schooled me in my emerging gaiety. Most importantly he introduced me to the world of theatre and ballet.

He had been born and raised in Colchester. After serving as a private in the desert army during the war, he had been a young actor and scenery painter with Donald Wolfit's renowned post-war touring Shakespearean company, immortalised in the play and film, *The Dresser*. Joe was in his late 40s and a leading light with the Colchester Operatic Society. He was the perfect companion at this time in my life.

I would never have met either of these gay men without 'cottaging'. It was absolutely the definitive gateway experience to a gay life in the 1950s.

8. My Very First Gay Pub

It was when I was in the fifth form in 1960, and I was just sixteen, that I came across the *Headgate* pub and realized that there could be more to gay life in Colchester than just 'cottaging'.

The *Headgate* was in the town centre opposite the bijou-like Cameo cinema that only screened foreign films, what were called then 'art' films, and the occasional X-rated very soft porn. It was where I first saw the films of Federico Fellini, beginning with his masterpiece of Roman decadence, *La Dolce Vita*.

It was not really a 'gay pub' in today's terms, but it was definitely gay friendly. In reality it was much more like a local hang-out for petty criminals, drug dealers – a newly emerging species on the scene – and other somewhat shady types. The landlord went by the gloriously spot-on name of Mr Lawless.

We 'poufs' and 'queers' fitted right in there to that low-life outlaw mould – in scenes almost as Felliniesque as those on the small screen across the street. The pub was also a magnet for those older camp followers and their prey – the curious, or perhaps bi-curious, National Service 'squaddie' lads in this major garrison town.

Lawless was always much too busy keeping an eye on his raffish customers to tumble to an underage drinker like me. In any case I looked older and had become adept at adding on a few years to my real age to pass as over eighteen. Letting on to my real age to the men I met usually resulted in being dropped like the proverbial 'hot potato' for fear of them being caught with a minor. Of course there were those who were turned on by my real age – or if I was extra naughty, by subtracting a few years.

Shockingly in those days people often turned a blind eye to paedophilia – save for the occasional sensational stories in the more prurient press like the *News of the World*. These usually revolved around a happily married scoutmaster leading a nasty double life, or a wicked vicar and his choirboy charges. The good old Ancient Greek term of 'ephebophilia' – lover of young lads would be more appropriate in my case.

Those titillating Sunday reads were about young boys, not strapping lads of sixteen. In fact sixteen was the typical starting age for Piccadilly rent boys – as I found later in my Soho outings with Messrs Wirth-Miller and Bacon. There was nothing like the present outcry today, where those meddling with minors have their houses daubed with the word 'pedo'.

It was a great relief when in 1962, I finally became legal – at least to buy alcohol in a pub. It was another five years before the law was at last passed to make gay sex legal – and then only for those over the age of twenty-one, within the privacy of one's home, between no more than two participants. Group 'cottaging' scenes, or homosex al fresco was still off limits. The valiant efforts of campaigners like Peter Wildeblood and my later good friend the prominent eye surgeon, Patrick Trevor-Roper, and the recommendations in the *Wolfenden Report*, had finally paid off.

My artist friend, Joe, was a regular at the Headgate and had told me tasty tales of its transgressive denizens, but he never risked breaking the law by taking me there himself and I never asked him to. Whenever I bumped into him there we would exchange a knowing nod, but remain discrete.

On Saturday night there were always a few familiar 'cottage' faces among the regular patrons but this was 'queer' society on a much broader canvass. It encompassed a whole variety of us 'poufs', ranging from the campest 'nelly queen' type – even the occasional 'out' drag queen – to the 'butchest omee'. The perfectly named Snug Bar was Colchester gay action central, and there sipping gin and tonics most weekends were the town's most legendary gayest residents, bosom buddies, or 'sisters' as they liked to be called – Cyril and George.

Cyril was a ladies hairdresser and George was in display (or 'on display', as Cyril would quip), dressing the windows at Bonds, the department store on High Street. Cyril wore 'slap', the gay slang for make-up – just ever such discreet eye shadow and a touch of the palest lipstick was his thing.

He had the daring, but sometimes personally dangerous habit of cozying up to any lonely looking military lad with the immortal opening line, "Just call me Gracie, dear." I only ever once saw him taught a lesson, when the object of his infatuation punched him in the face. Then for a week or so he just brushed it off by using more eye shadow to match and cover up his black eye. The *Headgate* was my first exposure to 'slap and camp' and I was always amazed that such overt seduction ploys seemed to work.

After being treated to a few drinks many a teenage trooper was hauled back to Cyril's home for a spot of motherly same-sex initiation, and perhaps a cup of cocoa, before they had to get back to the barracks for curfew time. Money may have changed hands for services rendered, but I am sure nothing on the scale I later witnessed between Dilly rent-boys and their punters in Soho pubs.

George was lean, dapper and goateed. He was the first man I ever saw wearing blue jeans. It is hard today to believe their comparative rarity then. Corduroy twill trousers were most often the casual wear of choice in the late 1950s, as the import explosion of American style blue jeans was still a few years away. They came in a deluge by the 1960s with every young person wearing them.

He ordered them and the briefest of underwear and slim-fit T-shirts from the Vince Men's catalogue. The catalogue published twice per annum was eagerly awaited by provincial gays with its parade of dishy scantily dressed, well endowed 'dolly boy' models. It was the nearest thing to 'wank' material in those days long before gay porn magazines.

59

Vince's actual shop was tucked away behind Regent Street on Foubert's Place, a passage-way that cut through to Carnaby Street – long before that street became the retail emblem of Swinging Sixties London. It may have been the only place in the world to buy sexy men's underwear in the distinctly un-gay times of the big Y-front – and long before men's briefs became a staple at every branch of M&S.

It was to Vince's that Denis Wirth-Miller took me on our first shopping trip, after he had taken me to buy expensive lime-scented shaving cologne at Trumpers. Trumpers were the barbers by appointment to HRH Prince Philip, right opposite that towelled retreat for upper-class gay patrons, the Jermyn Street Turkish Baths. Vince's was the first place I was ever asked by a touchy-feely salesman, while I was being shoe-horned into a very tight pair of jeans, whether I dressed to the left, or right. Is there anyone who really cares nowadays?

The shop and its mail order delivery were responsible for an almost serious 'outing' moment for me at school. Prefects, and by then I was one, always sat at the head of mealtime tables. During breakfast a junior boy was delegated to fetch the morning's post – yes, it always came early in those days – for me to distribute to the other boys sitting at my table.

Foolishly one morning I opened a bulky parcel addressed to me, instead of waiting until I got back to the privacy of my room. Out tumbled a trove of differently coloured very scanty briefs, direct from Vince's – it was, according to the note inside, another of Denis's wooing gifts. I had a lot of explaining to do at that breakfast table – something along the lines of it being a mistaken mislabelled delivery meant for a lady somewhere. I told Denis never to mail order presents to me ever again.

George was most definitely into lads younger than Cyril's 'squaddie' conquests, though he never showed any particular interest in me. He did invite me to tea once and proudly showed me his Vince catalogue and then did a fashion strut in his latest purchases. However he told me, rather like Francis Bacon did a year later, that I was much too sophisticated and knowing for his tastes. But Bacon typically also added damningly that I lacked 'dirty enough fingernails' for him. That was when I sadly accepted I could never convincingly pass for 'rough trade'.

But let's get back to George. He had some artistic talents that ranged far beyond window display. Long before those legendry rock star groupie chicks in California, George practised the erotic art of penis plaster casting. This was a skill that turned into sex shop big business in the 1970s when you could order a life size replica dildo moulded from the latest hung porn star's dick.

Tragically it all went awry for George one calamitous Sunday afternoon. Fatally pre-occupied with the size of a young lad's member he forgot the essential Vaseline undercoat while casting a couple of fourteen year-olds' willies. The resulting pubic hair imbroglio became a major scandal when the boys had to be rushed to the local hospital A&E to be cut free. The boy's parents, their school (not mine) and George's employers, were all informed. But the episode, although it became a Colchester gay legend, was hushed up to avoid a Sunday tabloid front page scandal and the display artist quickly left town. His friend, Cyril, beat a speedy retreat by moving to London to work at the trendy hair salon newly opened by Vidal Sassoon and his mum.

The *Headgate* itself has had quite a chequered history. In the 17th century it was called *The Ship*. By 1869 its licence had been withdrawn a number of times because of police reports of 'bad characters' drinking in the establishment. In 1876 it was renamed the *Elephant and Castle* and then in 1900 it finally became the *Headgate*. It retained that name for almost a century and then in a fit of local historical patriotism in 1981, it was changed again to *Boadicea*, to honour Colchester's very

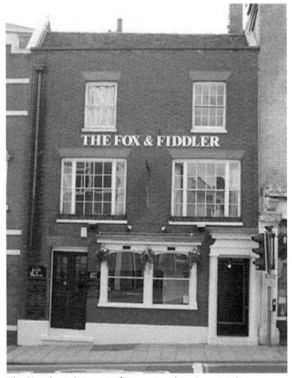

The Headgate's twenty-first century's re-incarnation.

own warrior queen. Almost fitting for a pub that had seen so much 'queenly' high heeled footfall in the past. However in 1997, it was bought by an outfit called the Really Good Pub Company and given the innocuous sounding name of *The Fox and Fiddler*. It is now, of course, a pale shadow of its previous raunchy and transgressive self.

9. Dramatics – Thespian Confessions

While I was at Whitchurch House I always ended up playing female roles, save for an early attempt as the King in some outdoor scenes from *Richard III* – no doubt influenced by a 1955 school outing to the cinema to see the great Sir Larry (Olivier) as the over the top deformed baddie. I can't remember how much I limped, but I know I made full-shock use of my semi-amputated left hand. My actual first Shakespearean part was playing a servant in an outdoor amateur production of *Romeo and Juliet* across the river in Pangbourne. The headmaster's wife had put me up for it.

Romeo was played by a very young Alan Bates. He had been a recent student at RADA and was now doing his compulsory National Service stint in the RAF, before returning to the theatre as Cliff, in the original Royal Court 1956 production of *Look Back in Anger*. It was a role that propelled this sexually conflicted actor to stage and screen stardom. Eight years later in my second term at LAMDA, by an extraordinary coincidence, I found myself living in a basement flat a few doors down from him. Earls Terrace, set just back from Kensington High Street, was a veritable gay enclave stuffed with theatre folk, including the identical twin playwright brothers, Peter and Anthony Shaffer, the early opera specialist conductor, Raymond Leppard, and Richard Chamberlain of *Doctor Kildare* fame. The terrace was owned by the Shaffer brother's father.

Bates was living with his secret lover, the actor Peter Wyngarde, who was to become a late 1960s TV favourite as the campy bouffant-haired lady killer sleuth in *Jason King*. Wyngarde was considerably older than Bates. It was a destructive relationship, not helped by the growing success of the younger actor. He always denied their intimacy. One could see them arguing, as their ground floor flat front windows were visible from the street.

I was 'picked-up' by them both on separate occasions but to avoid jealous scenes always kept mum that I had been with the other one. Unlike my earlier encounter with an even more famous actor they were sexy and a lot of fun. I used to regale friends with my tales of wrestling naked with hairy hunk Bates – long before Oliver Reed's turn, in the iconic homoerotic fireside scene in Ken Russell's *Women in Love*.

Wyngarde's career took a disastrous dip after his 'cottaging' arrest in the toilets at Gloucester Bus Station was widely publicised in the tabloids. He became known by the distinctly unappealing camp sobriquet of Petunia Winegum but lived to the ripe old age of ninety-four. Bates however, managed to keep his gayness under wraps including a long relationship with the Olympic ice skating star, John Curry – with the help of a marriage to the hippy actress, Victoria Ward. They had twin sons but she developed serious mental health problems after the pregnancy. She eventually was sectioned and died in 1992 of a heart attack. They had long before separated but did not divorce.

Tristan, one of the twin sons, died of a heroin overdose in a Tokyo public toilet. Curry, after a post-Olympic career as an ice ballet star, was an AIDS casualty in 1994. The Alan Bates biography, *Otherwise Engaged* by Derek Spotto, states that Curry died at his mother's house in Bates' arms. Despite so much personal sadness Bates managed always to give stage and screen performances of a dramatic range and a number superior to even his RADA contemporaries Tom Courtney and Albert Finney. I last bumped into him in New York in 1972 when I went backstage to see my old LAMDA chum, Richard O'Callaghan, who was co-starring with Bates in his Tony award winning performance in Simon Gray's *Butley* on Broadway. He invited me to have dinner with him at Sardis.

Alan was very amused when I told him that I had had a long sexual relationship with his fellow actor and friend, Peter

"Light thickens and the crow makes wing to the rooky wood." Me as Macbeth.

Alan Bates – my naughty neighbour!

Woodthorpe. Peter had played Aston to Bates' Mick, in the original production of Pinter's *The Caretaker* and also was Estragon in Peter Hall's original English production of Becket's *Waiting for Godot*. He became well known to TV audiences in the recurring role of the pathologist, Max, in the *Inspector Morse* BBC TV series. I originally met him in the legendary all night toilets at Marylebone Station just before I went to New

York. When Peter himself was later playing on Broadway I introduced him to the 'poppers' infused delights of the St Marks Baths in the East Village. So different from my earlier more furtive experiences at the Gentleman's Turkish Baths in Paddington, or the camply named 'Our Lady of Bermondsey Steam Baths'. Gay men flocked there on Saturdays to scrub up with the butch dockers as they came off shift. Southwark and much of working class housing was typically without bathrooms in those days.

My own theatrical bent followed a dual path when I was a teenager. At the Grammar School I progressed from playing Brutus's servant in *Julius Caesar*, to Malvolio in *Twelfth Night*, Dick Dudgeon in Shaw's *The Devil's Disciple*, and the Donald Wolfit role of the Jesuit Father Provincial in *The Strong Are Lonely* – an obscure play about Spanish missionaries in Paraguay in 1760s that was the basis later for the Jeremy Irons/Robert Di Nero 1986 flop movie, *The Mission*. At the school I directed a number of plays and entertainments, including an outdoor production of *Romeo and Juliet*. This time I got to play Romeo and not Juliet. In 1962, my last year at CRGS, I reached my Shakespearean pinnacle by playing the title role in *Macbeth*, and soon after won a scholarship to LAMDA, one of the country's leading drama schools.

In 1959 I joined the Junior Drama League – my family were by then living near London in Walton-on-Thames. JDL was an acting workshop for teenagers, run under the auspices of the British Drama League in Fitzroy Square. The Christmas and Easter holiday sessions culminated in an annual residential Summer School where we spent three weeks rehearsing a full scale production. I came a cropper in 1961 at the Bangor University Summer School. I had been cast in the role of Maria's brother, Bernardo, in *West Side Story* directed by Clifford Williams, who later became an associate director at the Royal Shakespeare Company.

Dancing was definitely not my forte – George Chakaris I was not. Insufficiently warmed-up and during a run through of the Dance at the Gym scene, I landed awkwardly and broke my lower left leg in two places. The break echoed round the rehearsal hall like a pistol shot and looking down I saw my left lower leg at right angles to my knee. I spent a morbid Bank Holiday weekend in a Bangor hospital ward overflowing with motorbike casualties – where the ward sister implored me as I was fully conscious, to comfort the seriously injured and dying brain damaged biker boys. There was no helmet law then.

I was ferried back by train to my parent's house in Walton-on-Thames. It was a somewhat ignominious trip home; loaded on to luggage trolleys into a series of guard's vans and then being carried shoulder high on a stretcher through concerned evening rush hour commuters at Waterloo Station. It reminded me of the story about Vivien Leigh, petrified of flying, comatose on sedatives being stretcher loaded on to transatlantic planes.

Back at school that autumn term, my leg in plaster, I auditioned for a new segment of Anglia TV's local news magazine. They were looking for a teenage interviewer for a spot once a week called, *Youth Wants to Know*. I got the job and in rotation with a young schoolgirl from Ipswich, from Christmas until the end of the summer term made a fortnightly regular appearance. The novel format was to have a school-age teen interviewing an East Anglian celebrity, or person of local importance. I interviewed a parade of eminent locals, notably the incredible but snobby, Barbara Cartland, who arrived at the studio with three furs – a big fur coat to step from the chauffeur driven car in, a fur cape while in make-up, and a mink stole on camera. "Young man, you are far too young to understand the meaning of love and romance", she purred in her upper-class voice – entirely innocent of my blooming sex life, one that was definitely not of the Mills & Boone variety.

I also interviewed two gay local big shots, Sir Frederick

Me as the seedy music agent in 'Expresso Bongo' – JDL 1961.

Ashton, the Royal Ballet's chief choreographer, and my dear old friend, Dudley Narborough, the bishop of Colchester. Another eminence was Clement Freud, the celebrity chef, broadcaster and finally Liberal MP for Ely, who was exposed as a serial abuser of very underage girls after his death. I was rolling in pocket money as I earned fifty pounds an appearance, plus hotel expenses – which I never used for hotels. I simply caught the late evening train back to Colchester from the studios in Norwich. It was only just over an hour's journey. Despite it being a great experience there was a downside. Being on the local telly so regularly made me something of a celebrity and I was often recognised in the street. It meant one thing – a temporary halt to my 'cottaging' escapades.

It was during one of these JDL school holidays that I paid a visit to the 'cottage' at Gloucester Road Tube Station. I had discovered it some years before while staying in London with my Prep School friend, Dudley Davenport. It was there that I had an encounter with a very big 'movie star'. Lingering at the urinals I found myself being cruised by no other than the matinee idol and heartthrob star of the *Doctor in the House* series, Dirk Bogarde. It turned into one of the most bizarre pick-ups I ever experienced.

He beckoned me out to the street and asked if I would like to come home with him. We went to a flat in a mansion block just around the corner from the station in Ashburn Place. He seemed to have a problem using the keys and I surmised that it might not be his own flat, but one probably on loan from a friend. I had read in a film magazine that he actually shared a country estate house in Amersham with his agent friend Tony Forwood, the ex-husband of actress, Glynis Johns; it was a relationship he always denied was anything but platonic, despite the rumours that persisted throughout his career on the gay grapevine. In those days it was a certain career death for stars to be openly gay. All the Hollywood gay greats, like Rock Hudson and Cary Grant, sensibly had studio arranged sham marriages.

Once we were inside his manner became even more curious when he realised that I was aware of his identity. He informed me that whatever I might be thinking he was, in fact, not Dirk Bogarde but just the stand-in the film studios used to set-up camera angles. I said nothing knowing that while stand-ins

70

were often used they were unlikely to be the exact double of the star. There followed a perfunctory series of awkward sex acts that lacked anything like the recent passionate performance I had seen him give with Olivia de Havilland in *Libel* – a film whose plot strangely also revolves around a case of mistaken identity. It was one of the most disappointing sex scenes of my life up to then. So thank goodness for the star-power performances given by Alan Bates some years later.

JDL had a formative and lasting effect on my life. I met a group of people who remain best friends until this day. Two of the tutors at Summer Schools – Norman Ayrton and Kristin Linklater were also on the faculty at LAMDA. They played an important part in my training, and later in my theatre life in New York also became as good friends. Norman became the principal at LAMDA after I left – but re-entered my life again when he fetched up as an instructor at the Juilliard School in New York, America's premier post-graduate drama, music and opera academy.

I had been Norman's assistant when he directed Joan Sutherland in a very early career performance as Cleopatra in Handel's *Giulio Cesare*, at Sadlers Wells Theatre in 1963. Vivid memories of the dress rehearsal – where to make the somewhat heavyset diva glamorous, we had her carried by four Nubian slaves on a palanquin, with a live baby leopard sprawled across her lap. It peed all over her of course, and so it had to go. Sutherland would stand in the wings waiting for her entrance swapping filthy stories in her rich Aussie accent, then sale on to the stage with exquisite Italian coloratura. She was, of course, sensational.

Kristin was the daughter of the novelist Eric Linklater and became one of the world's leading voice coaches. She was also a professor in the Theatre Division at Columbia University. We were neighbours and pioneers in a then run-down East Village before it became gentrified and ultra-expensive. She remains

Professor Emeritus at Columbia, but semi-retired runs a residential summer Voice Centre on the Isle of Orkney. Norman died in 2017 at Denville Hall, the renowned nursing home for ailing theatricals at the end of their lives. He was 92. My old friend Peggy Mount had similarly spent her last days there too.

10. Gay Bishops, Assorted Clerics and Other Queer Characters

Long before the various brouhahas in the Church of England and its ambiguous dealings with the friends of Dorothy brigade, Colchester had its very own gay bishop. The Rt. Reverend Dudley Narborough, after time as the Provost of Southark Cathedral and a wartime ministry in the blitz-proof crypt of St Martin's in the Fields, arrived to tend a flock in Colchester and its rural environs. Trafalgar Square's loss was our town's gain.

He exchanged the crypt's soup kitchen and wartime refuge for servicemen for a life of pastoral care diocesan duties and his complete emersion in the cultural and educational life of life of the area. Dudley was short of stature, jovial with twinkling eyes and a heavy smoker. Immensely popular throughout his time as bishop he soon augmented his clerical duties by becoming not only the chairman of the governing board of the Grammar School, but also for the thriving Colchester Repertory Theatre as well. He was also the patron of many local charities including his pet project, the restoration orientated, Friends of Essex Churches.

I first met him when Jack Elam, our very perceptive headmaster, chose me as the perfect match to be his escort on Sports Day in 1959. It was obvious from the start as I guided him around the various track and field events that 'the Bish' had a very ancient Greek Games take and appreciation of the youthful sporting prowess on display. He must have clocked me as a fellow traveller, as he was completely unguarded in his praise of the older lad's physiques. An invitation to a glass of sherry that evening in his official residence, a large ramshackle Edwardian house on The Avenue, cemented a firm and lasting friendship.

While I remained at the school in the Sixth form he

Dudley Narborough, Bishop of Colchester from 1946-1966.

encouraged me to bring a group of my particular friends to the house, where he entertained us without a trace of predatory intent. The only possible dodgy moment was the obligatory acceptance of an almost benedictory kiss on the forehead at the end of the evening. He may have admired boys but it was expressed in a very AE Houseman manner towards us Essex lads. In keeping with that poet's Shropshire bunch there were never any sexual overtures. These were preserved for the more attractive of the young actors at his other official position, the Rep. I always wonder if Harold Pinter, who was an actor there in the early 1950s with the stage name David Baron, ever used Dudley's predilections in his later plays?

He took a special liking to my boarding house best friend, Brian Ashen, and even deputised him as his personal chaplain and later driver for his confirmation duties round the county. Brian nursed Dudley when he became seriously incapacitated during a short retirement and he was left the car and a small legacy when he died in 1966. Brian was the first of my Old Colcestrian 'gay plague' casualties in 1989.

Dudley was great chums with Marjorie Allingham, one of the great crime writer queens along with Agatha Christie and Ngaio Marsh, in that post-war golden age of detective fiction. She had just had a substantial success when I met her with *The Tiger in the Smoke*, featuring her sleuth creation, Albert Campion. He appears in most of her thrillers and became the eponymous hero of a much watched BBC TV series in the 1980s, played by Peter Davison, a future *Dr Who*. JK Rowling, of *Harry Potter* fame, says it is her favourite detective novel.

He took me to dinner several times at the house she shared in Tolleshunt Darcy, near Maldon, with her husband the illustrator, Philip Youngman Carter. A navy commander in the war, he was by now mostly confined to bed with chronic gout where he convalesced by dabbling in prize-winning needle point. It seemed to me a strange hobby for a straight man, but later on I met several gay men who swore by its potency as a relaxing activity.

They were avid Tory supporters and had promoted Aubrey Moody, a friend of theirs and Dudley's, as the local party candidate. He ran and lost against Tom Driberg, the dynamic, but notoriously 'queer' Labour candidate in Maldon, during the momentous post-war election in 1945 when that party swept Churchill from power. Allingham and her husband were vehemently anti-gay as was standard then, and I heard them use very homophobic slurs against Driberg. It puzzled me that they never seemed aware of Dudley and Aubrey's identical proclivities. But it was a very different world then and only a very few brave 'out' souls broadcast their sexual preferences in those prejudiced days. Aubrey decided that politics was not for him and trained for the Church of England priesthood.

Aubrey had taken a shine to me when Dudley took me to his vicarage in Feering, near Marks Tey. His gentle feyness belied his bravery and exploits as a highly decorated wartime commando for which he was awarded the Military Cross. I spent several chaste weekends with him and he gave me the most expensive birthday present I had ever received, until I met Denis Wirth-Miller – a gold framed eighteenth century colour print of Shakespeare's Globe Theatre.

He introduced me to the Hon. Geoffrey Browne, a member of the wealthy Guinness family, who took me to that High Anglican Mecca, St Mary's Bourne Street, near Sloane Square. It was stuffed with incense and bell loving high church queens. That particular parish would play an important part in my life when I later taught drama at Tulse Hill, a London boy's comprehensive school. My best gay friend and fellow teacher at the school, Trevor Richardson, and his long term partner, John Greenhalgh, worshipped there.

John later crossed over to normalcy while I was in New York, got married and brought up his family in Pimlico when he became the church's sacristan. Edna, his wife, is now a very good friend of mine. Both John and Trevor, who became an Anglican vicar in Kings Cross, and then moved over to Rome and became a parish priest in Norfolk, died of cancers some years ago.

Geoffrey Brown ran an agency called InterChurch Travel that arranged pilgrimages and religious orientated trips throughout Europe and to the Holy Land. He sublet his flat in Covent Garden to me in the summer holidays of 1961 before I returned for my last year at the school. I had saved plenty of money from my weekly interviewing gig on the Anglia TV show and was busy auditioning for drama academies. It was my first attempt at living alone – so it was in some ways an audition for life.

The flat was slap bang in the middle of the gayest part of London's West End. It was on Long Acre, a stone's throw from that favourite haunt of gays and theatricals, or both, the *Salisbury* pub. From the second story window there was a grandstand view of a very busy 'cottage' in the alleyway opposite. I am sure that is why Geoffrey had chosen to live there.

The flat had previously been owned by James Agate, the eminent theatre critic for the *Sunday Times*. It still had an elaborate pulley system set into the bathroom ceiling installed for kinky sex scenes with his favourite rent lads – the Palace guardsmen from the Knightsbridge barracks who needed to supplement their meagre military pay.

Dudley was a very middle of the road Anglican and did not really go in for 'smells and bells' but he enjoyed the company of high churchmen – like Tom Driberg, the notorious 'cottaging' MP. We went to lunch several times at his picturesque house, Bradwell Lodge, besides the River Blackwell in his Maldon constituency. Despite a couple of initial gropes when he chased me round the dining room table I don't think he really fancied me. He probably thought I was too posh for his 'rough trade' tastes – rather like George the plaster-caster, and later Francis Bacon.

Driberg had practically invented the modern gossip column when before the war he worked for the *Daily Express*. He was not only a good friend of Cambridge spy and fellow cottager, Guy Burgess – he had also been a communist at university – but also the infamous East End gangster twins, the Krays. One of the twins, Ronnie, was for Driberg's part conveniently also gay.

They pimped for him and another well known 'queer' parliamentarian, Lord Robert Boothby. Boothby played both sides of the fence and was the lover of Prime Minister Harold Macmillan's wife! The Krays provided the two of them with 'rough trade' working class boys from the East End. I soon got used to the idea that upper-class gay men seemed to have 'a thing' for lower-class lads, not middle-class well spoken lads like me.

I never got to meet the Krays but am sure I would not have been Ronnie's type. However, when later I was teaching at the London boy's comprehensive school, my star acting pupil Alan took me to meet his parents just before he went up to university.

His mother turned out to be the sister of the Kray's major rivals – the South London gangsters, the Richardson brothers. More vicious than even the Krays, they had the charming habit of nailing a squealer informant's feet to the floorboards.

Driberg had numerous brushes with the law – sensationally being once caught giving a blow-job to an off duty parliamentary policeman in the underground toilets by

Tom Driberg, the notorious 'cottaging' Labour MP.

Westminster Bridge. Luckily he was always shielded by Lord Beaverbook, the press baron proprietor of his gossip column's *Daily Express*, and senior members of the Metropolitan Police, who either shared his sexual interests, or enjoyed his political patronage. The paper was immensely successful, the largest circulation tabloid in those days.

He had a sham marriage as a cover for his outrageously dangerous queer behaviour. His wife was completely aware of his other life but settled for the prestige of being married to a powerful MP. He even rose to become chairman of the Labour Party. Eventually his political luck ran out and he lost his seat. He was made a life peer in 1975 as Baron Bradwell. But a few months later he had a fatal heart attack in a taxi en route to the House of Lords from his flat in the Barbican. As recently as 2016 there were startling revelations in the press that the Director of Public Prosecutions in 1968 had, for political reasons (Harold Wilson or Lord Beaverbrook?), halted investigations about Driberg and Lord Boothby's procurement of underage East End boys.

Another of Aubrey Moody's chums was an East End clergyman, a scion of the famous sherry and port importers, Sandeman's. He was responsible for ferrying coach loads of underprivileged East End lads to a dodgy campsite in the Essex countryside. It was rumoured that the much required recreation for these needy youths, desperate for fresh air and fun, was often more depraved than deprived. I now realize that all these boy-loving clergy, politicians and upper class 'pervs' must have been part of a network. What the Sunday tabloids would have called a 'TOFF'S SECRET KID VICE RING', if they had ever got wind of it. I don't think Bishop Dudley was totally aware of some of his friend's pervy tendencies and the goings on in the diocese. He would not have approved as he never showed the slightest bit of interest in young boys himself.

I met another leading member of the Church of England hierarchy through Dudley, the charismatic Mervyn Stockwood, Bishop of Southwark. He sat in the House of Lords, was something of a maverick and was very outspoken in his support for homosexual law reform. *Private Eye*, with it's typical right-wing nastiness at that time, openly referred to him as 'Merv the Perv'. He had a reputation for being gay, and indeed his bishop's residence overlooked the 'cruisiest' part of Tooting common.

He never cruised me but being a good Welsh socialist from Bridgend he was intrigued when I told him about my Cardiff family and the fact my father's father had worked all his life in Tiger Bay docks as a shipping broker. He even made a joke about the Bay's most celebrated progeny, Shirley Bassey. Then I told him that my father's cousin went to school with Richard Burton and he was eating out of my hand. He asked his housekeeper to bring another bottle of wine to the lunch table and started to regale us with tales of boozy evenings with his regal buddies, the Queen Mum and Princess Margaret.

Brian and I were frequently taken by Dudley to visit the absolute love of his life, Norman Millard, Archdeacon of Oakham and a resident canon of Peterborough Cathedral. They had met at Oxford as undergraduates in 1919, in a moment described by Dudley as almost pure EM Forster. From the window of his room at Worcester College he spied a tall handsome rowing blue advancing across the quadrangle – a still dripping oar resting on muscular shoulders. Dudley set out to seduce this 'butch' dreamboater and they remained lovers for the rest of their lives. Norman played a valuable role for gay rights when he was deputised to give supportive evidence on behalf of the Church to the parliamentary Wolfenden Committee considering the legalization of homosexuality and female prostitution.

He owned a vicious little Jack Russell terrier called Patch. It was part of the resident canon's duties, armed with a big torch and using Patch, to flush out the courting couples canoodling in the Cathedral Close at night. I remember suggesting to him that he should adapt a song from the popular Rogers & Hammerstein musical, *South Pacific*: "Hello young lovers – you're under arrest!" He was amused but I don't think he used it. The poor old dog was also given to bouts of very smelly flatulence and once while we were eating supper, sitting under the table, he passed some particularly stinky wind. Edith,

Mervyn Stockwood, Bishop of Southwark from 1959-1980.

Norman's housekeeper leapt up and yelled, "Patch has farted – cover the butter." Forever after it became a long running jokey line for Brian and me at countless dinner parties.

There was no one quite like Dudley, the 'Bish'. Maybe there was gossip but there was never any real hint of scandal associated with him. He was the perfect mentor, with no fear of predation, and through his valuable friendship I met a cast of fascinating queer, in both senses of the word, and odd characters. He was genuinely loved by his flock and even today more than half a century since his death if you Google him you will find the legend: "Dear old Dudley Narborough, Bishop of Colchester – a more out and out old steamer was never seen."

He would no doubt have been amused that the cleric that replaced him as Bishop was named Coote – although definitely not, as they used to say, 'as queer as a coot', he was a happily married family man.

11. Artistic Licence: Joseph Robinson

Until I was sixteen my gay life was mostly restricted to adventures of the 'cottaging' kind. There were liaisons less dangerous with theatre folk from the local Rep Company and my new best friend, Joseph Robinson – mentor, struggling artist and doyen of the Colchester Operatic Society. He had picked me up in one of the Castle Park toilets. I was fifteen but told him I was seventeen to avoid any alarm on his part.

I spent most Sunday afternoons at tea in his basement flat on Wellesley Road, about five minutes away from the school. Brian Ashen, my best boarder friend, would sometimes tag along as well. The fledgling sex, at the start of our relationship, gradually gave way to something much more worthwhile and fascinating; a complete education in the arts with particular emphasis on theatre and dance. To be honest I was never truly turned on by Joe physically but his knowledge and personal experience in all these arts was something I really appreciated. It was also great fun in the one-upmanship stakes to be smug when a teacher incredulously asked me, "How do you know that, Hughes?"

Joe gave me all the most valuable insights a gay teenager could want. He was particularly informative about the history of gaiety, from the lad-loving Ancient Greeks right up to the recent scandalous court case involving Lord Montagu of Beaulieu. He was accused of 'indecency' with some National Service airmen and before that with boy scouts camping – in the tented sense! – on his estate. The backlash from this case resulted, in 1957, with a group of the more progressive politicians of all parties and some sympathetic Anglican churchmen setting up the Wolfenden Committee. Its remit was to examine the possible path to the 'legalization of homosexual acts between consenting adults'. Its positive recommendations were not passed into law for another ten years by the then

Joseph Robinson's pencil portrait of me at 15.

Wilson led Labour government. I was already twenty-five and had been illegal all those intervening years!

I don't think I realized, until much later, how 'struggling' Joe actually was and how big a hole in his budget providing a slap-up tea for one and sometimes two growing lads it might have been. There was always a spread of toasted crumpets, sandwiches, cakes and sometimes even a glass of wine. I like to think we made up for it years later when we had him up to stay in our London flat and treated him to the theatre, or the ballet and dinner in one of our favourite Soho restaurants.

Joe was always jealous of my other rather ritzy artist friend, Denis Wirth-Miller. Denis would later play a major part in my climb up the gay social ladder. So I learned to give Joe a somewhat edited version of my wild but wonderful times with

Denis and his metropolitan miscreants. Looking back Joe was the much more wholesome person of the two, without a doubt. But lashings of the licentious, or even just a soupcon of 'delicious debauchery' – as in Joe's favourite saying, was delightful fun for a growing gay boy.

I soon met Joe's London best mates, a gay couple, Andy and Frank. Andy helped Joe out financially by finding him freelance jobs – art restoration work, or portrait painting commissions. Frank was much younger than Andy and very sexy in that special 'Essex Boy' way. He was a gym teacher at a boy's secondary school in Romford. They remained my friends and when I moved to London naughtily set me up for a brief affair with their friend the noted actor, Robert Flemyng. Flemyng was known for his leading West End roles in the plays of Terence Rattigan and Noel Coward, the prominent gay dramatists of that time; and also stiff-upper lip parts in those popular wartime films of the 1950s. Flemyng was divorced and had an actress daughter. He was a very closeted but discreet queer – like most actors I met in those days.

Joe introduced me to his best local running buddy, Seley Little, a closeted gay librarian who moonlighted as the main theatre critic on our local paper, *The Essex County Standard*. The Rep was weekly and it was closed for an August break and the popular Christmas Panto ran for two weeks. Seley must have written at least forty-five reviews a year. This on top of amateur shows, the Operatic Society's annual bonanza often starring Joe, and then the glowing write-ups he gave my performances in the school plays. His twin sister, Beth Chatto, became the champion Chelsea Flower Show Gold Prize winner ten times and a distinguished writer about innovative non-fancy gardening. She sent me a charming letter when he died. She lived on until 2018, aged 94.

In 1986, living in New York, I became concerned when Joe stopped answering my letters. Transatlantic telephone calls were expensive then and had to be made through an operator but I tried to call and was told that his line had been disconnected. I got in touch with the new curate at St Peter's Church on North Hill. The same church we all attended on Sundays from the boarding house. The summer before he had been a theological exchange-student volunteer at a children's summer camp in East Harlem I was supervising. He wrote back to me with a ghastly story. Joe had been chased by a young mob of 'queer bashers' into the middle of traffic on the High Street, where he was hit by a lorry. He never regained consciousness and died a few days in the Essex County Hospital, just along Lexden Road from the school.

There was a long overdue retrospective exhibition in 2011 of his portraits, World War Two Western Desert sketches of his soldier comrades, and theatre and ballet designs at the Minories Art Gallery in Colchester. I emailed the curators to ask if I could contribute an appreciative essay of my friend and mentor in the catalogue, explaining his positive influence on an isolated gay teenager. I was given the cold shoulder. However, a most prized possession is the pencil portrait he drew of me aged fifteen that you will find illustrated in this memoir.

12. Glitter and be Gay: Denis Wirth-Miller

One fateful summer evening, in the public loo at the bottom of North Hill, I was picked-up by yet another local artist. Denis Wirth-Miller changed my provincial gay teenage life for ever. It was he – the notorious 'queer' artist that Joe had warned me about. A member of the celebrated post-war Suffolk/Essex border 'bohemian' set, Denis lived in Wivenhoe with his longtime partner, Richard (Dickie) Chopping, the illustrator best known at that time for his *trompe l'oeil* jackets for Ian Fleming's best selling *James Bond* novels.

Wivenhoe was a sleepy little fishing port at the mouth of the River Colne – the same river that ran through Castle Park in Colchester. This was before the new University of Essex arrived and changed the town for ever. Seley Little, my theatre critic friend also lived there, as later did Francis Bacon, both on the appropriately named Queen Street. Actress Joan Hickson lived in the town well before her break through fame as the original TV Miss Marple.

In fact Wivenhoe was as full of intrigue as Agatha Christie's St Mary Mead, minus the murder count. The ghastly political hack and TV personality, Peregrine Worsthorne, had a weekend cottage rented from Denis and Dickie at the top of their garden. They intensely disliked him, but appreciated the steady income from his rent. He became editor of *The Sunday Telegraph* and was noted for his frequent journalistic homophobic sneers. He was the same interviewer who famously forced Ian McKellen to 'out' himself on a BBC radio programme in 1988.

That night Denis whisked me from the toilet to their Wivenhoe home, the Storehouse, a converted warehouse on the River Colne quayside. Dickie was away that night at their London flat in Montpellier Street, opposite Harrods – as well as working as an illustrator he was on the teaching faculty at the Royal College of Art. There followed eighteen chock-full months of relentless courtship from Denis as he took me on a glittering grand tour of rich gay men's country houses, fancy Soho restaurants, Piccadilly rent boy pubs, after-hours drinking dives like Muriel Belcher's Colony Room, and the seedy notorious Harrow Road Turkish Baths in Paddington.

After the Second World War the Essex-Suffolk border with its pretty villages and quaint little towns became bohemian gay central. In easy reach of London it became a magnet for an emerging group of 'queer' artists, writers and their friends and hangers-on. House prices were cheap and homes were snapped-up to become the venue for wicked weekend house-parties. The area's apex arrived when the original celebrity chef and *Sunday Times Magazine* food writer, Robert Carrier, renovated crumbling Hintlesham Hall and turned it into a shrine for cuisine with a distinctly chi-chi accent.

This new age of gaiety very much revolved around Dickie and Denis's quayside home. In those grey post-war years they became known for their 'gloom-busting regattas' as their friend Frances Partridge, the diarist and last standing member of the original Bloomsbury set, called them. In her late 1940s diaries she wrote vivid descriptions of the Wivenhoe gay 'goings-on', as she was a frequent visitor to their house. She also collaborated with Dickie when she provided the text for his exquisitely illustrated series of Shell nature books.

Another visitor was her close friend Janetta Jackson. She had married Derek Jackson, the bizarre bisexual atomic scientist, racing car driver and part owner of the *News of the World*. They had divorced by the time we met. With her divorce settlement she bought the terraced house in Montpelier Square where Dickie and Denis had their basement *pied a terre*. Denis threw a seventeenth birthday party for me there – caviar and champagne and a host of grand guests; among them Francis Bacon, ITV broadcaster Daniel Farson and Janetta's other ex-husband, the TV journalist Robert Kee from *Panorama*.

Partridge's birthday present to me was a copy of her son Burgo's badly written but shocking recent book, *A History of Orgies*. The party was something else, while not exactly an orgy, it was an extraordinary baptism into this new brave world for an innocent (?) young lad from Colchester.

I am not quite sure how I managed to separate my two lives – grammar school boy by day and Denis's feted teenage discovery at night – but I did. It helped that my parents were safely tucked away in Washington DC and officially when not at school in Colchester, I was in the care of my Nan in Winchester.

Denis juggled things so that we were in Wivenhoe when Dickie was in London and vice versa. A lot of time was spent with his best friend, Francis Bacon. I will never forget my first visit to the Bacon studio and flat near South Ken Tube station. There was one sparsely furnished main room with a big divan bed covered in a Moroccan rug lit by a solitary light bulb – the signature image in many of his paintings; a kitchen with what looked like a brand new but seldom used stove, a fridge stuffed with champagne and pâtés, and right in the middle of the kitchen, a bathtub. The toilet was out in the hallway. The studio itself was a cluttered cramped dump of canvases, painting materials, and walls plastered with violent images, torn from picture magazines – along with a selection of photos of animal and humans in motion by the nineteenth-century photographer, Eadweard Muybridge.

He gave me his phone number once when Denis was in the loo. But it was obvious from the one time I went to see him alone that I was not his cup of tea. Wrong accent; not into smacking him around; and fingernails too clean.

They took me to their favourite pricey Soho eating places: Chez Victor, London's celebrated oldest French restaurant on lower Wardour Street. There you might find yourself sitting at a table next to the likes of Yul Brynner, or Vivien Leigh. Or the equally star-studded Old Compton Street branch of Wilton's, London's oldest seafood restaurant. Both were within easy reach of Francis and Denis's best-loved alcohol pit stop – Muriel Belcher's infamous after-hours club, the Colony Room.

To reach the bilious green painted bar you had to pass through a downstairs dustbin strewn hallway on Dean Street and then climb a smelly staircase. Muriel imperiously presided, perched on a stool at the end of the bar, just inside the door – insulting her clientele with an entertaining range of obscene banter.

She always called Denis 'Denise, dearie'; Francis was for ever addressed as 'My daughter'; I was 'Denise's schoolboy bait' and everybody else was 'Cunty this', or 'Cunty that'. Carmel, Muriel's attractive Jamaican girlfriend, served behind the bar along with Ian Board, who was known as 'Ida'. Ian inherited the club when Muriel died in 1979.

Muriel always said that 'cunt' might be a term of abuse but 'cunty' was a term of affection. Rather like the drag queens of the time she would often feminize her terms of address and so even the butchest of Bacon's East End 'rough-trade' conquests might become 'Miss Thing'. This transplanted 'handsome Jewish Brummie dyke', as George Melly described her, may not have been as witty as Oscar Wilde, but she was the past-mistress of camp innuendo. But even she might have fallen off her stool, when Bacon's portrait of her sold for nearly £14 million in 2007. It would have been more than enough for all the frequent times 'Lady Bountiful' Bacon treated the entire bar to champagne.

The bar was a lure for the artistic *demi-monde* and assorted Soho deadbeats of that time. Everybody seemed to be either gay, or perpetually drunk, or both. I learned to water down my drinks from the bottles of Vichy water on the bar in order to avoid getting drunk. George Melly, the jazz musician and critic, and the painter Lucian Freud, brother of my interviewee

Clement, were often propping up the bar. The Freuds were the grandsons of Sigmund. I wonder what psycho diagnosis he would have made of Muriel's club.

I met William Burroughs, the drug-loving American writer of the *Naked Lunch*, then living in London at Muriel's. Later, when I moved to New York, I found him living just round the corner from my East Village apartment. My cruising buddy and neighbour, the photographer Robert Mapplethorpe, was very enamored with him. We used to go to the Burroughs apartment, a converted YMCA gym locker-room on the Bowery. He told us he loved living there as he could still detect the odour of sweaty jock straps!

My absolute favourite of Denis's friends was the young black lawyer and sometime actor, Paul Danquah, who lived with his lover, Peter Pollock. Peter was heir to the Accles and Pollock bicycle metal tubing company. They had a flat overlooking Battersea Park. Paul's father had been a minister in the Ghana government of Kwame Nkrumah but with an opposition then in power was in prison awaiting execution. He had a fling with film director Tony Richardson, Vanessa Redgrave's bisexual husband. He cast him as the cute horny black sailor who impregnates Rita Tushingham's character Jo in the film version of the Shelaugh Delaney play, *A Taste of Honey*.

It was a serious piece of non-type casting; acting was not his real forte and after a few small TV parts he forsook acting and became a lawyer with the World Bank in Washington. We had a very sexy illicit tryst in a broom cupboard in their flat while Pollock, Bacon and Denis were out of their drunken minds in the front room.

I kept in touch with him and last saw him at a Nina Simone concert in New York. They were buddies and he took me round to the great jazz diva's dressing room afterwards – it was one of the musical highlights of my life. Paul died in Tangier, where he and Pollock had lived since the 1970s, at the grand old age of

90 in 2015. He was almost the last of my Wirth-Miller connections to pass.

The lights on this gay 1950's pantheon may have dimmed somewhat. Who now remembers many of those luminaries I met through Denis? Painters like John Minton and the perpetually kilted camp Scottish artist double-act, 'the Roberts' McBride and Colquhoun, all denizens of Muriel's bar. Bacon and Freud the only remaining Titans, both now deceased, joust from their graves for the ultimate prize of whose paintings will reach the highest sales value.

Few people read the novels of Angus Wilson now, a leading novelist of those times and another of Denis's friends. He lived with his probation officer lover, Tony Garrettt, not far from Wivenhoe just over the Suffolk border. I vividly remember the first time I was taken to meet Angus in his cottage at Felsham and my surprise when a ginger wigged vision in full Elizabethan drag opened the front door. The distinguished novelist was Good Queen Bess in a cross-dressed rehearsal for the local drag ball.

It was the gay Essex/Suffolk border's campest season highlight thrown annually by a quartet of London's society queens who shared a very secluded house in the aptly named Sible Hedingham. Angus and Tony rented the nearby cottage from their friend and neighbour, Patrick Trevor Roper, the Harley Street eye surgeon and brother of historian, Hugh. I had a minor fling with Pat behind Denis's back but re-engaged with him thirty-one years later at an AIDS conference in New York. He was one of the three very brave and openly homosexual witnesses to the Wolfenden committee. Pat became an early gay rights activist in the 1960s and was instrumental with others in the founding of the UK AIDS charity, the Terrence Higgins Trust.

When I returned to live in England I decided to catch up with my past.

In March 2002 I took the train to Wivenhoe. First, I went to

Queen Street to see Seley. He was completely bedridden, obviously ailing and being looked after by a live-in carer paid for by his twin sister, Beth Chatto. We chatted about our memories – Joe Robinson and those halcyon days of the old Colchester Rep when the company presented a new production each week; and his rave reviews for my sterling performances in the school plays. It was hard going as he seemed to tire very quickly and so I said my goodbyes promising to be in touch. It had been a difficult and sad conversation for me.

Then I went down to the Quay and rang the bell at the Storehouse. A carer here also answered the door and let me in. She announced me as, 'this young man whose been living in New York'. I was almost sixty! "I don't know any young men from New York", someone said, and a blind, and very decrepit Dickie, shuffled in out of the gloom. He did not recognize me until I told him. "It's me, Tim Hughes."

"You..." Dickie said, "that boy who gave me such heartache all those years ago!"

The once brilliant illustrator, the man that Zandra Rhodes told me had taught her to draw, was definitely not thrilled to see me.

We had always had a very awkward relationship ever since the day he came back unexpectedly early from London and found a precocious sixteen year-old being sponged-bathed by Denis in their ornate bathroom with all its framed nineteenth century post cards of Vesuvius erupting into the Bay of Naples. This time he nearly erupted himself, as my unexpected presence was obviously very upsetting. "I suppose you want to see Denis... well you can find him up at the post office getting his pension." Then he stumbled back into the kitchen. "Don't worry about him", the carer, knowing nothing about our past, said as she let me out. "He talks to me like that – he's very rude to everybody."

I turned the corner from the Quay and climbed slowly up High Street. I had forgotten how steep it was and had to stop and use my puffer to get my breath back. In the post office I found a disorientated and shriveled old man looking like a very ancient and decaying Stan Laurel, with an oversize NHS issue hearing aid wound round his right ear. It was Denis. Difficult to reconcile this image with the eager posh-speaking queen who had picked me up in the toilet at the by-pass roundabout on North Hill, all those years ago.

It took some time for my former mentor to recognize me. I had last seen him in 1980 on one of my flying visits from New York. He took me to lunch at one of the restaurants that had sprung up since the arrival of the new University of Essex in nearby Wivenhoe Park and regaled me with stories of his conquests of the young male students. I had written to him a few weeks previously to say I was planning to visit and now I knew why I had not received a reply. He managed to tell me that he had to go home to wait for a car lift to the hospital. I imagined his indignity at being crammed into a car, with a lot of other ailing senior citizens en route to the clinics at the Essex County Hospital, on Lexden Road.

He had once told me that after I left the Grammar School, which was almost adjacent to the hospital, he sometimes used to sit in his car and watch the flood of boys in purple blazers streaming out onto Lexden Road when school broke-up for the day. Denis had made something of a fetish of those purple blazers and had insisted on doing a series of portraits of me wearing nothing but one of them. I recalled the awkward time he had insisted on going to Owen Wards, the school outfitters, to try on blazers to find his size.

I told the incredulous assistant that Denis was an old boy and was looking to give his school contemporaries a surprise on Old Boy's Day. I don't think he swallowed that one but it did not get in the way of his typical 1950's shop assistant servility and he sold Denis a blazer. Nowadays I am sure he would have called the police, or at least rung the school, as soon as we had

Denis Wirth-Miller (left) with Francis Bacon.

left the shop to report this strange camp older man with a
schoolboy in tow.

Denis was able to tell me that he sometimes had bouts of
dementia. I could see that the effort of trying to remember
things was making him nervous. So I walked him slowly back to
the Quay half expecting to bump into Miss Marple; or even that
first editor of the *Sunday Telegraph*. Pompous posh Peregrine
Worsthorne whose biography recalls the scandalous drunken
goings-on of his 'queer landlords', Dickie and Denis and 'their
notorious queer painter friend, Francis Bacon.' I left him waiting
for his hospital lift at the Storehouse door and walked back to the
station through streets now crammed with trendy eateries,
boutiques and even a delicatessen. On the train back I felt
immensely sad. I realized that it was probably the last time I
would see Seley, Denis, or the still resentful Dickie ever again.

The lights on my 'Wivenhoe set' have dimmed a great deal
since that sad day of my final visit. In February 2004 I saw an
obituary for Frances Partridge – she died at the great age of one
hundred and three. Pat Trevor Roper died a few months later in
his late eighties. I knew about his pioneering gay rights activism
but had no idea that he had established a series of eye hospitals
in Africa. Bacon had already died years before from a heart

attack in Madrid in 1992. His paintings sell for eye-watering amounts – the triptych portrait of his rival Lucien Freud sold for £90 million. Yet his best friend Denis's paintings can be picked up for as little as £500, despite several being in Her Majesty's Private Collection.

Denis and Dickie had been the first local gay couple to have a civil partnership, celebrated at the Colchester registry office, in December 2005. Just over two years later Dickie died. He was found in a bad way on the Storehouse floor by Daniel Chapman, a true friend, who had been caring devotedly for these two men in their final years of extreme illness. Denis in his incapable state of dementia had had not been able to help his lover of over sixty years, failing to even call an ambulance.

Denis himself died two years later in 2010, deranged, raving and sometimes restrained to a hospital bed. It was the same hospital that my other artist friend, Joe, had died in twenty-two years before. Daniel telephoned me to tell me the sad news. Deservedly he inherited the Storehouse and told me I was welcome to visit any time I liked.

So along with Joe's fatal encounter with the homophobic thugs it was a grisly end for both my artist friends and mentors from those far off teenage 'cottaging' days. When I was last in Colchester at the school for the theatre opening ceremony, in memory of my drama teacher, I took a tour of the town. I found all my cruising landmarks had gone, casualties of the town council's shrinking budgets, or perhaps even closed in an attempt to deter any transgressive hanky-panky of the gay kind.

Epilogue: More of an Intermission

While writing this memoir of my growing-up gay – predominately the teenage years from 1954 until I left school in 1962 – I have often projected people and places forward, as I found it impossible to stay in the linear moments of just the past. I think the afterlife of events is always interesting and so I hope you will forgive me for having jumped ahead so often – after all everybody reading a good book wants to know what happened next.

Most of the characters from those early years are long gone but in the immortal words of the song from Stephen Sondheim's *Follies*, "I'm still here."

After leaving the Grammar School I went to LAMDA on an Essex County Major Scholarship.

It was there that I finally faced the truth about the 'deformity' that had proved so handy (sic) playing Richard III. Visits to the theatre became a torture as I became obsessed watching an actor's hand movements, instead of following the play.

It was no good believing the kindly LAMDA tutor, who thought she was being helpful when she suggested I could always join the BBC Drama Company, a kind of radio repertory company, "where no one will see your hand". That sounded a bit like the 'consolation prize' to me. Fortunately Norman Ayrton, the vice-principal, had a better idea. "Why not become a director," he suggested. "You had lots of experience at school. Get a job as an assistant somewhere in Rep and in a few years time you could also come back here and teach."

My new friend the actor David Dodimead introduced me to his agent, Elspeth Cochrane. She had been James Mason's secretary and had recently set up an agency called THEATRE WORKS. This lovely lady sent me to the Arts Theatre in Ipswich. She already represented the then novice actors, Ian McKellen and Edward Fox, who were in that Ipswich company.

I stayed there for three seasons as assistant to both the

director and the general manager, but also directed several productions in my own right each season. I did a daring double bill for that time of Genet's *The Maids* and Pinter's *The Collection*; and the Royal Shakespeare Company's anthology about England's kings and queens, *The Hollow Crown*. I also directed that Rep perennial, Agatha Christie's thriller, *The Hollow*, with Philip Voss and the hilarious Maggie Jones who became a *Coronation Street* matriarchal legend. Maggie had written the best audition letter ever: 'I am getting tired of playing only nuns and prostitutes...' Most importantly I directed Peggy Mount, of ITV's comedy series *The Larkins* fame, in an English translation of a 1893 German play, *The Beaver Coat* by Gerhart Hauptmann.

During my time there I was approached by the head of English at nearby Wolverstone Hall School – the boarding grammar school for bright boys with difficult home situations, run by the Inner London Education Authority (ILEA). He asked me to teach drama there for one day a week. My star pupil was Mark Wing-Davey, son of the initial *EastEnders* matriarch, Anna Wing. He was later in the original *Hitchhiker's Guide to the Galaxy* and is now head of the drama department at NYU, where I studied for my Master's degree in Social Work. It was at Wolverstone Hall that I was spotted by John Welsh, the ILEA's chief drama inspector.

I had always played both sides of the sexual divide with numerous girlfriends during my teenage years. Then at the theatre in Ipswich I had a short affair with one of the assistant stage managers, Maureen Race. 'Mo' was already involved in a long-term relationship with Christopher D'Oyly John, who was co-incidentally working with my friend Jim Acheson on Dr Who. She became pregnant with our son, Adam, but chose to return to London to marry Chris. We settled on a pact which meant I would step aside from any connection with them, or my son.

Over the years I was haunted by thoughts of Adam and in

2013 I eventually gave in and Googled Chris. I discovered that he had died of cancer in Eastbourne in 2009 and had a widow called Penny. Weirdly there was no mention of Mo, or Adam. With such an unusual last name I soon found Adam. He was living near Eastbourne in Bexhill-on Sea and working as a dementia carer. I wrote to him and amazingly he telephoned me back the next day. There followed a month of communications without me owning-up to his paternity. But he must have put two and two together and one day called to ask if I was his father. It was the most emotional conversation of my life. We soon met-up and have become marvellous friends. I adore him and curse myself for not breaking the pact years ago. He feels the same way but teases me that I only came looking for him – so I would have the perfect carer in my demented old age.

When I left Ipswich John Welsh secured me the position as head of drama at Tulse Hill Boys' School, one of London's first comprehensives. Up the hill from Brixton it was a new six-storey building with lifts, in the glass and concrete go-to brutalist style of the late 1950's. Old boys included that thorn in Maggie Thatcher's side, Ken Livingstone, who became the first mayor of London and the eminent actors, Kenneth Cranham and Tim Roth. I did lavish productions of *Hamlet* and *Romeo and Juliet* and a modern dress version of Ben Jonson's *The Alchemist* set in Brixton Market, all with the considerable help of my old CRGS chum, James Acheson, who purloined costumes for me from the BBC wardrobe. He was designing *Dr Who*. Working at Tulse Hill was one of the happiest experiences of my life.

Then the rules changed and one could no longer be qualified to teach using merely a professional diploma – like the one in drama I had earned at LAMDA. It meant that I had to go back to college and study for a teaching certificate granted by the London University Institute of Education.

Three years of weary grind as I retraced all I already knew about inspiring kids in the magical world of theatre. Fortunately the boredom was broken by a former history teaching colleague from Tulse Hill. Robert Lacey, who was now an editor on the Sunday Times, asked me to submit an undercover report on the Piccadilly rent boy scene. In the next three years teacher training took a back seat to part-time media and journalism projects.

The rent boy report proved too racy to run for the *Sunday Times*' easily shockable breakfast readers as they tucked in to their porridge, toast and marmalade and it was spiked. *Piccadilly Profiles* re-surfaced when a few months later it ran in *Jeremy*, the brand new magazine for a gay readership. In September 1969 I joined the magazine as an associate editor under Lacey's editorship. It was the world's first gay publication of this kind and glossy into the bargain. Among my many assignments was spending an extraordinary two weeks with the then struggling young singer David Bowie, long before his iconic status truly set in. He came out as a bisexual in the piece I wrote – a first. Ironically, David never repaid me the money he borrowed once for an Indian meal.

Looking back now I feel somewhat disappointed in myself at *Jeremy* – it is obvious from re-reading my articles that I was writing as an observer of gay life, not as a genuine gay man.

In another slice of inauthenticity, Robert, who was not gay, edited the magazine under a pseudonym. He later wrote the best selling biography of our dear Queen, *Majesty*, swapping one kind of close quarter queen watching for the real thing, as he became ITV's and CNN's premier contributing 'royal watcher'. But I am for ever grateful to him for the chance he gave me to get into journalism. And besides, my mother thought he was one of the handsomest men she had ever met when we bumped into him one day in Cambridge. What a waste for the world of gaiety.

Meanwhile back in my part-time teacher training I could deploy the talented students at Trent Park College as actors. I directed a very early stage production of Orton's radio play,

Ruffian on the Stair and the second British production of
Spring Awakening by Frank Wedekind. It had been produced
previously by the Royal Court Theatre for one Sunday night
club production only to skirt the Lord Chamberlain's obscenity
ban. He objected to the teen sex galore and the schoolboys'
'circle-jerk' scene.

One night at the Coleherne I met a very sexy young American.
Jerry Denlinger was of Polish stock from Ohio and worked as an
international ceramics buyer for Macy's, the huge NYC
department store. I hauled him back to my flat for a night of red
hot passion. He was returning to America on a morning flight
and so I figured it would be the bog-standard one-night stand.
Later in the morning he called me from the airport to say that
dense fog had cancelled his flight and could he camp out with
me. The fog lasted for two more days and I was hooked.

Over the next few months Jerry, unusually for a Yank, wrote
me letters – lots of them. He persuaded me to up-sticks and
move to New York to be with him. As soon as I had taken my
finals I did. It was now 1971.

Jerry betrayed me with a Brooklyn Italian Mafioso gay guy,
Dino, who kept phoning and threatening to break my legs. I
moved out but instead of returning to London I decided to stay
and try my luck in New York. I had met some interesting new
friends and fallen in love with the city's post-Stonewall 'out and
proud' gay world. Luckily I was able to secure a position
teaching drama at CUNY, the City University of New York. It
was in their special off-site projects department and I began
under their auspices to teach eager prisoners at the Brooklyn
House of Detention and amazingly adventurous senior citizens
at their centre in Queens.

That was just the beginning of nearly thirty tumultuous years
as a green carder in New York. There was my introduction to
the druggy 70s, including my own wonderful experiences –
thanks to Mr Huxley and his opening of the 'doors of

perception'. I started my own theatre company, the Downtown Theater Project and guest directed plays for several other outfits running the gambit from Shakespeare to Alan Aykbourne. I was most proud of premiering all the very queer plays of my outrageous and stroppy friend, Carl Morse. I had two fabulous lovers, Bill O'Banion, a nurse who became a Los Angeles hospital's senior administrator – to my eternal shame I let him down most terribly; and Guy Paulin, the couturier who took me rather unsuccessfully to Paris to live; and then I met the real love of my life, an amazing 'wetback' (illegal alien) Mexican artistic genius, Enrique Luna. Mr 'Henry Moon' was the only lover I did not meet initially in a gay bar – see, I had moved on from 'cottaging' – but as a blind date, courtesy of my faithful

Mr 'Henry Moon' – Enrique Luna.

friend, Tamara Bliss, who sometimes wrote music for my New York productions.

Then came the gay plague and I lost all my lovers and so many friends. I went back to college at NYU and trained as a counsellor and social worker at night, while working by day at the Peter Krueger HIV/AIDS clinic at Beth Israel Medical Center.

But I have overreached myself in this over-long epilogue to those teenage times and if dear reader you have survived my prose as far as this, you might look forward to a fuller account in the forthcoming *Fairy Tales of London Town & New York City*.

Lightning Source UK Ltd.
Milton Keynes UK
UKHW021832070920
369493UK00015B/1283